P9-DBR-918

NOBODY'S IN TOWN

BOOKS BY EDNA FERBER

Short Stories

NOBODY'S IN TOWN
BUTTERED SIDE DOWN
CHEERFUL—BY REQUEST
HALF PORTIONS GIGOLO
MOTHER KNOWS BEST
THEY BROUGHT THEIR WOMEN

The Emma McChesney Stories

ROAST BEEF MEDIUM
PERSONALITY PLUS
EMMA MCCHESNEY & COMPANY

Novels

DAWN O'HARA
FANNY HERSELF THE GIRLS
SO BIG SHOW BOAT CIMARRON
AMERICAN BEAUTY
COME AND GET IT

Plays

THE ROYAL FAMILY
(with George S. Kaufman)
MINICK
(with George S. Kaufman)
DINNER AT EIGHT
(with George S. Kaufman)
$1200 A YEAR
(with Newman Levy)
STAGE DOOR
(with George S. Kaufman)

EDNA FERBER
Nobody's
in
Town
DOUBLEDAY, DORAN & CO., INC.
New York 1938

PRINTED AT THE *Country Life Press*, GARDEN CITY, N. Y., U. S. A.

F
F 373N

COPYRIGHT, 1937, 1938
BY EDNA FERBER
ALL RIGHTS RESERVED

CL

66650 a

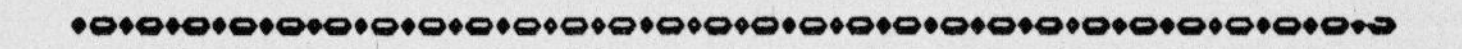

CONTENTS

NOBODY'S IN TOWN

NOBODY'S IN TOWN

ONLY LAST WEEK it had been cool—cold, really. Yesterday had been merely warmish. But this! This was it. Mrs. Alan Career, waking at eight, knew at once. Her nostrils, bred to New York City's effluvia, sensed hot rubber, melting tar, sunburned gasoline and oil; poisonous gases, blazing heat on brick and stone and steel; murk shot through with smoky sun. Born in the East Sixties (streets, not years) she knew that summer had come to New York.

They had predicted a cold summer. A lot they knew about it, the idiots. Just because May had been bearable, and the first two weeks in June. She had stripped the apartment down to the airy essentials. She had replenished the broken set of tall frosty glasses meant for iced tea and mint juleps and Tom Collinses. And she went about saying, as she had said every June for the past five years, "I simply adore New York in the summer. It's so restful. The roof restaurants and the air-cooled movies and Long Island week ends; and first thing you know it's September and everyone's coming back half dead and their skin looking like potato chips."

"Really!" her women friends said. "I must try it some time. We're sailing Wednesday. Bark wants to motor through France and Italy; and then we'll have two weeks in Salzburg for the Festival."

Every time she left the apartment there were piles of luggage downstairs in the foyer or at the curb—smart beige bags with brilliant red and green and yellow sashes painted about their middles, and little luxurious dressing cases softly jacketed in buff. Tags and labels read Queen Mary—Normandie—Rex.

Always noisy, there now was a new rush in the streets, a louder buzz in the air, stronger vibrations underground. A roaring of airplanes overhead. The engines of vast ships turned, and their rudders churned the bay. The hum of a million motorcars filled the countryside. Automobiles darted and swept up the lanes of New England or nosed toward Colorado and California and Canada. At Pennsylvania and Grand Central stations the crowds milled like stampeding cattle.

Day by day, bit by bit, as the blasting heat continued unabated, New York cast off her French corsets, sent her furs to cold storage, took off her hat, rolled her stockings. Ungirdled, in bare legs and sandals, she let the hot odorous breezes from the Hudson and the East River blow through her hair. The great proud apartment buildings fell into their long summer sleep. One by one they pulled down the shades and awnings that were the eyelids over their hard bright window eyes and allowed themselves to be draped in their summer shrouds of slip covers. Their guardians relaxed. The doorman unfastened the two top buttons of his taupe-and-blue summer uniform. Superintendents, usually so dapper and double-breasted, could be detected lurking in the shadows of foyer pillars in shirt sleeves and no collar. The big old brownstone houses and the newer Georgian pink bricks and the vast white marble palaces on Fifth Avenue and Park and the East Sixties and Seventies were boarded up tight with only little crescent moons showing in doors and windows like slits of eyes squinting suspiciously down upon the rare passerby.

One by one, furtively, almost fearfully, the Little People now crept out of their tenements, their walk-ups, their fire-escape flats, and claimed the New York which was rightly theirs. Gratefully they poured into the parks and squares whose grass they watered, whose gravel they raked, whose shrubs and trees they planted, whose walks they swept. They wandered free in the proud streets whose homes they lighted, whose food they supplied and delivered. You saw them sprawled on the courageous grass, timidly displaying their clean worn undergarments to an understanding world. Their tired unlovely feet were bared to the sun and wind. Their gray-white skin knew the ardor of the elements. Gangs of kids in ragged knickers and limp shirts and nothing beneath these yelped along the avenues; urchins in bathing trunks followed in the blessed wake of the sprinkling cart. They poured out to the streets, the fire escapes, the parks, the L trains, the subways, the beaches, benches, squares, curbs, roofs, doorsteps—the six and a half millions of people left in deserted New York.

And now, for the first time, you saw the contours of the city, no longer winter-choked. Its bone structure was there; its ribs and muscles stood out. It was like an overfat person from whom the excess weight has been peeled, pound by pound, so that now at last the actual body may be seen in its real outline, stripped and lean.

That second week in July the Alan Careers had it out at the breakfast table. Usually Patty Career had her breakfast in bed, but she said it was too horribly hot to have it there—to have it anywhere. She sipped her iced orange juice and glanced at her *Herald Tribune*. He sipped his iced orange juice and read the *Times* front-page headlines and glanced at the market, saving his more intensive perusal for the subway.

It was eight-thirty in the morning, it was hot, it was hell, it was unbearable. Patty Career burst out with it though she had meant to wait until evening. Hysteria, probably, induced by heat and sleeplessness; and intensified by certain Talks with her mother.

She set her glass down now with a queer little clatter and pushed aside her plate of thin toast so that it executed quite a nice little spin. "Look, Alan, I can't stand this any longer. Honestly I can't. I can't face another summer in New York."

He looked at her over his paper. Then he put it aside altogether. She went on with a rush now. It had been pent up for weeks.

"Everybody's gone this year. Everybody! During the Depression it was—we all—I didn't mind so much—practically all our friends in the same fix. But now it's different. The Depression seems to be over for everyone but us. It isn't fair. It isn't fair to me or to Susan."

Susan had been born very mathematically, so that she was now four. Her appearance had coincided with the vogue for quaint old-fashioned names bestowed by rather hard-bitten modern parents. All Susan's little friends were named Susan, Ann, Jane, Mary, Kate, Prue, Betsy.

Alan Career's mouth was now etched with lines that one would expect to see on the face of an embattled man of fifty rather than on one of thirty-three.

The past ten years had done some very odd art work on the faces of Alan Career's generation. "Two more years," he now said, as though he had said it to himself many times, "and I'll be out of the woods."

"Who knows what 'll happen in two more years! I'll be dead, for one thing, and Susan too, probably, in this poisonous heat and gas."

"Oh, now, listen, Patty. It isn't as bad as that. I can manage a couple of weeks somewhere up in the mountains, or Maine. There are little cabins. This heat won't last."

"Oh, Alan, for heaven's sake! Little cabins! Tourist camps, I suppose."

Now it was he who pushed back his plate with unnecessary force. "We could afford something better if we didn't live beyond our means. If we didn't live in this damned silly expensive apartment we might clear out for a couple of months in the summer. But you can't live anywhere but the East Sixties or Seventies. Why! It's the ugliest stone-pile in the world. A million people like you trying to edge into it because it's fashionable. Fashionable! It's a ghetto of the rich and people like us who are pretending to be rich. We're a couple of young people trying to get along. Hell! Why don't we live like it! We pay thirty-two hundred a year for this stinking little third-floor back apartment, and that's why we can't have a house in the country or a trip to wherever it is you want to go. Why! What for!"

She now spoke in very controlled tones, using her broadest New York accent with a tinge of London. Alan Career hailed originally from Chillicothe, Ohio. "I always have lived in this section of New York. One naturally is accustomed to having a decent place in which to receive one's friends."

"If they're friends they'll come if you're living up in Fordham. As for most of the gang that comes here to eat our dinners and guzzle my whiskey all winter so that we can go there and eat their dinners—it's a merry-go-round—it's silly—it's idiotic!"

"Will you please not shout so that Dahlia and Miss Mapes will think we're quarreling."

"We are."

"Perhaps you are. I'm not. I'm simply trying to talk to you like an intelligent adult. For one thing, living here is good for your business. And Susan's future depends on her making the right social contacts——"

"Susan!" he now yelled. "My God, the kid's four years old! The right social contacts for an infant just out of diapers."

"Isn't it just about time that you lost your Ohio viewpoint, Alan? When I was four my mother——"

"A lot of good it did her. What did it get you? You had dancing school and Miss-Gipp's-on-the-Hudson and all the Right People and Southampton and your picture in the rotogravures and when you grew up you married a hick from Ohio who can't even afford to take two months off in the summer. Maybe if you hadn't made the right social contacts you'd have married a millionaire or the King."

"He doesn't care for women under forty," Patty reminded him icily.

"You knew I had a few thousand dollars and a job with a future and not another damned thing. Why did you marry me? I didn't try to put anything over on you or your family."

"I married you because I was crazy about you."

"Well, I'm just what I was then; a boy from the

Middle West trying to make good in the Big Town."

"No, you're not. That's the trouble with you Midwestern men. You all have adolescent Abraham Lincoln complexes and go around with your mental socks rolled down, and black string ties and square-toed Congress boots inside you."

He turned back his coat to show her the label stitched on the lining. It was dated. "Nineteen thirty-two. But Betzel made it and it cost me one hundred and thirty-five bucks."

"I know, I know. But dated clothes aren't so amusing any more. The time is past when it was considered chic to be poor and stay home and get your evening clothes at Macy's. But everything's going to be brocade and fur and lumps of gold next winter. You can't get a box at the opera for love or money."

"Thank God."

"Here. Look at this." She picked up her *Herald Tribune* and pointed with one forefinger tipped by its cool coral nail to a line at the head of that paper's society gossip column.

The summer exodus is complete, it read. New York is deserted. Nobody's in Town.

"That's pretty silly. There are millions of people in New York all summer."

"Don't quibble, Alan. There's nobody that counts. Nobody important."

He pushed back his chair, stood up. "Well, what 'll we do about it, Patty? I'm not holding out on you. I'll do anything I can. I wish to God I could——"

She brought it out, then, with a little rush.

"Mother has offered to take Susan and me to Europe for the rest of the summer. And even Miss Mapes, if she'll take a cut in wages. A lot of Mother's stocks and things have come back. She got some reservations through Bill Snowden's pull and all—of course I told her if you absolutely—but I was sure you'd—the Champlain sails Thursday—I think it's just wonderful of her, but if you——"

"Yeh, wonderful." Dully. Then, as though the words had just penetrated his consciousness, "Thursday! You mean this Thursday! That's day after tomorrow!"

"Well, I sort of—after Mother asked me I sort of—not packed, but went over things."

"I see."

So then, quite amazingly, it was tomorrow and immediately it was Thursday and in a moment Patty and Susan became two little specks among hundreds of other specks that were growing smaller and smaller as the distance between the French Line dock and the Champlain's deck rail widened. He felt very odd and alone standing there among the perspiring close-packed crowd massed at the pier end, waving and shouting futile last-minute messages. He turned and made his way through the throng. They looked a good deal like the people who had sailed, he thought. Nobody that counts. Nobody important.

The ship had timed its sailing with the tide. As Alan Career looked at his watch he saw that the afternoon was gone. It was hardly worth while going back to the office, except for the afternoon mail, and Miss Voss could take care of that, unless it was something colossal. Fine chance of that in the middle of July, end of the week, end of the day. Good old Voss. Nobody important, eh? Well, she was pretty damned important, with a memory that never slipped up and a head for figures like an Einstein.

Her brisk, unlovely, reassuring voice on the telephone. "No, there isn't a thing, Mr. Career. The

Street's as dead as Trinity churchyard and the thermometer outside your window says ninety-nine. . . . I can take care of the mail, what there is . . . Kunz's is the only one that needs your signature and I can forge that . . . Newbold phoned and I told them fifty or no dice, like you said. . . . I made an appointment with Mr. De Palma for ten Tuesday because he's taking the plane, is that O.K.? . . . So whyn't you just go home and cool off? . . . Did the folks get away all right? I sent the fruit and all, and wired the purser. I hope everything's the way you wanted it. . . . Shall I phone your house you're on the way up?"

Good old Voss. Important, vital old Voss, who lived in the Bronx and would die in the Bronx, and who was to him as his own right hand. Back, he thought, to an empty flat, an empty town, an empty life. . . . Everything next winter is going to be brocade and fur and lumps of gold. . . . Maybe Friday night he'd pack a bag and go out to the Beach Club if Jay or somebody would put him up. Noisy bunch, though, and a lot of drinking. . . . Bet the apartment is an oven this time of day. . . . Warm and cold shower and a cold drink. . . . Wonder what Dahlia's got for dinner. No lunch, in the rush to clear things at the office before taking the girls to the boat.

He had been wrong. The apartment, when he had let himself in, was almost cool in comparison with the torrid streets. The shades were down, the windows shut. Dahlia had straightened and picked up and tidied after the flurry of packing and departure. What dignity and poise and intelligence behind those broad black features. Her face had worked comically, tragically, when she had said good-by to Susan, her darling. When she had come to work for them five years ago, at the beginning of their marriage, Patty had said, amused, "Dahlia? Your mother was fond of flowers, I suppose. Is that how she happened to name you Dahlia?" "No, ma'am," Dahlia had said in her calm rich voice. "It's out of the Bible, the one who was the wife of Samson."

Alan Career went into the bedroom and stripped. It was pleasant, walking around naked, no one in the house but Dahlia humming in the kitchen. The tiles of the bathroom floor were hot to his bare feet, and the perspiration was like a wet coat of oil all over his body. He'd have a lukewarm bath first and use some of Patty's scented bath salts like a big sissy and just lie in it, and then he'd have a shower, cool and cooler and cold and he'd stand under it for hours until his veins ran ice water and to hell with the doctors who said it was bad for you. Clean clothes and then a highball—no, a gin fizz or a julep with a big spray of mint stuck in the side of the glass. Boy! He might have it right now and wait half an hour for his bath. He wrapped a bath towel about his middle and padded to the swinging door of the pantry.

"Heh, Dahlia! Got any mint?"

"Any what?"

"Mint. To put in a julep. I'm parched."

Her dusky face was almost beautiful in its regret, its suffering. "Oh, Mr. Ca-reer! I ain't got a sprig. Not a sprig. Tell you what. I'll just skip over to Lexington get you a bunch of mint."

"Oh, never mind. It's too hot. Don't you bother."

"I'm going. When a person got their face fixed for mint, they want mint."

"Well, if you—uh—look, Dahlia, what 've you got for dinner? H'm?"

"What you want? What you got a hankering for?"

"Oh, it's late. It's probably too late to do anything about it now."

"Not onless you want roast beef or leg of lamb hot night like this, you don't. I can get it same time I'm getting the mint. Too late for what? What you want?"

"I know what I don't want. I don't want any of that damned cold jellied soup nor yet I don't want cold salmon with green sauce, that's Patty's idea of a—uh—Mrs. Career probably planned——"

Dahlia knew the male free and untrammeled. She threw her dinner menu to the winds. "Ain't that the truth, Mr. Career! That ain't vittles, it's like swallowing a lump of cold mud, it's bad for your stomach, any weather. What you got your mind fixed on, makes your mouth all spitty when you think of it? H'm?"

His voice took on a dreamy note as he leaned there in the doorway, the towel clutched around him. "Dahlia, I want soft-shell crabs, little ones, a million of them; and sweet corn, yellow bantam, cut off the cob and mixed up with butter and little green peppers. And I want French-fried potatoes, and then I want an enormous bowl—not a saucedish, but a bowl—of big red raspberries, cold and sugared so the sugar is kind of crusty. That, madam, is what Ah craves. Do you think you could get it?"

"It's as good as got," said Dahlia. Then a look came into her face. "When you're all through dinner and it tasted good, is it all right if I go uptown tonight right early after dinner?"

"Why not?"

He slapped back to the bathroom. He turned the cold water faucet all the way, and the hot water faucet one third. He turned them again. Nothing happened. He stared like one struck by nameless horror. No water. No water! He turned on the taps over the wash bowl then. Nothing. Grabbing the towel again he rushed toward the kitchen bawling, "Dahlia! Dahlia!" But he arrived there just in time to hear her friendly voice greeting the back elevator man and then the slam of the heavy metal door as they began to descend. He bounded to the house telephone which was at the side of the pantry door. "Look!" he shouted to the voice of the hall man who answered, "there's no water! What's the matter with this place on a day like—— Well, let me talk to the superintendent then. What's his name? The new man. Bauers. Let me talk to Bauers. . . . Hello? Is this the superintendent? You're the new man, aren't you? Well, what the hell kind of a note is this, anyway! No water, and a hundred in the shade!"

WATER

Brophy always said that many a millionaire would like to live where he spent the whole of his days, there in the stone house on a lake, with the breeze blowing through the park across the water, and always cool in summer and warm (or warm enough) in the winter. He called it his Town House. To the Board of Water Supply of the City of New York it was known as the South Gatehouse of the water supply system; and familiarly as the Central Park Reservoir. And there daily from eight to four Dan Brophy reigned a king and had for thirty-five years. At home in the crowded little flat on West Sixty-fifth there was the Old Lady, who was ailing, and Ellen and her husband and he always sore since he was out of a job and come to live with her folks; and their two little ones, and Katie who'd never married and religious cracked and forever in a corner with her beads. A man couldn't find a spot to sit with his paper and his pipe that there wasn't a screeching and pother and the Old Lady sitting there in her wheel chair with a look that turned your heart over. But here—here in the Park Gatehouse—all was peace and dignity and order and he loved it.

And now it was gone. By four o'clock this afternoon his robes would drop from him, his scepter would be taken from his hand, and he would be only an old man of seventy, out of a job. Seventy you were through, and they took your job away from you. Well, the young folks had to have their chance.

It was thirty-five years ago that Dan Brophy had got his papers as stationary engineer and come to take charge of the big Central Park Reservoir. He knew it better, he loved it more than any place on earth: the smooth fresh lake that was the reservoir water, the little stone house jutting into it. A little damp in the winter, perhaps, but you got used to it. He was supposed to come on at eight in the morning, but almost always he was there a little after seven, especially in the summertime. Dan Brophy was one of the hundreds who controlled the water fed to New York's millions. It gave him an enormous feeling of responsibility, power, importance.

And now young Noonan would take over tomorrow morning at eight. He was coming in this afternoon to get last-minute instructions from Dan Brophy. The night man came on at four. Noonan was to have been here by three. It was half-past, and after, and he wasn't here yet.

Dan Brophy didn't in the least look his seventy years. A slim tight little Irishman with a fine long head. He would have denied its looking more English than Irish. He always had color in his face; thin cheeks with the red rather high on the cheekbones, and lined but not wrinkled. His eyes were an unexpected hazel and they made you think of the eyes of an Irish setter; fine, faithful, trusting eyes. Thick iron-gray hair and a trim little gray mustache like a smart colonel's. He looked sound and clean and fresh, and he was.

New York politics had come and gone over his head—dirty politics and criminal administrations; crooked men and honest men of various breeds and stocks had held the vast rich city in their hands for a few years, but Dan Brophy had quietly gone on attending to the water that must always be on tap.

During his daily hours of work he ruled alone. No one was allowed within the Gatehouse without his permission. There were folding iron gates, so that you could leave the big wooden doors open and still be locked securely within. Daily his program was the same. First thing, at eight, he descended to the operating chamber far underground down in the bowels of the earth, to try out the motor. For thirty-five years he had done this at eight and never missed a day. Down the narrow spiral steps, round and round, sixty-one steps down, sixty-one steps up, a dozen times a day for thirty-five years. No wonder he had kept a nice flat stomach and never got winded like the inspector when he came his rounds, though he was forty and slim.

The reservoir was fed by the sweet waters of the Catskills. Dan liked to say it. The sweet waters of the Catskills, drinkable, washable, mixable. No copper in it. He knew all the names of the vast main reservoirs and the rivers and dams that fed the water to New York's millions, and he loved to tell them off. The kids—Nelly's kids, his married daughter—and before that his own kids used to ask him to say them and Nelly had made a kind of song out of the names to sing them to sleep when they were babies. Good hard-sounding Indian names, and Dutch, like music. He knew them all, without Nelly's song to guide.

Schoharie and Catskill and Mohawk,
Shandaken and Kaaterskill Creek,
Esopus and Croton, Kensico, Ashokan,
Hush now and the fairies will peek.

Byram, Jamaica, Richmond, Manhattan and Queens. Bronx. Silver Lake. The words were honey on his tongue.

This morning he had gone about his work as usual. He had seen that everything was in apple-pie order. The little stone house was cool and shady but when you stepped outside it was like putting your head in an oven. But he liked a taste of the sun now and then. It felt fine on his skin. Part of his job—assumed by himself—was to keep clipped and neat the little privet hedge that bordered the Gatehouse stone steps and coping. He liked clipping, snipping. Vaguely something stirred in him. A throwback, probably, to peasant or gardener ancestors in Ireland or England. He always had been handy with tools; clipping a hedge or seeing that an engine ran sweet and smooth, it was all one.

Brophy glanced at his control board. First Avenue—Second—Third. Fifth. Tenth. All in order. Here, on his left, the East Bay, there the West Bay, tidy little oblongs of water there below the flooring, like indoor swimming pools. And outside, through the rear door, open now, the shining silver expanse of the lake itself, the July sun glaring down upon it and the lake giving back as good as it sent.

There were all sorts of interesting things in that lake. Most of the people walking round the two-mile reservoir circular path didn't notice. Only he and the Regulars. He knew them and they knew him. There was Bernie Baruch and Groucho Marx and Greta Garbo and Gilbert Miller and Katharine Cornell and George M. Cohan and many another as famous. They knew him, and sometimes they stopped a moment to chat. Hello, Dan! How are you, Brophy! He had seen some of them grow from youth to middle age. He never presumed on his knowledge of them. Hard-working people, like himself, serious about their jobs and walking to refresh the strength that was in them, and recharge their batteries. He had seen them walking around the reservoir in sun and in snow, happy and in trouble; a sparkle in their eye or a glance that never left the pathway.

In the big lake itself there were all manner of living things but you didn't tell people about that because they wouldn't understand; they'd think they dirtied the water when really they kept it clean. There were turtles, for instance, and ducks and fish. Pike as big as your leg that had been there for years and years. And the pigeons and gulls that rode the water.

He had got into the way of talking aloud to himself. He stepped out now to the little balcony overhanging the lake, at the rear. Fifth Avenue to the east and Central Park West opposite—he had seen amazing things happen to those skylines. He had seen palaces go up and come down. There was Andy Carnegie's house at Fifth and Ninetieth still standing. Few enough of them left now. When he first came on gatekeeper the whole of Fifth Avenue was nothing but fine big houses—the Vanderbilts and Goulds and Astors. Gone now, and square stone apartment houses, twenty stories high, in their places.

He minded the day they had come to take down the little iron fence dated 1858 that ran all the way around the reservoir stone coping. A nice neat little fence. Victorian, they called it, after the old girl herself, doubtless, though that was queer here in America. They had carted it away and put up an ugly wire fence in its place, eight feet high and hideous, to keep people from throwing themselves in the water, they said. A lot of good that had done. If a person wanted to kill himself bad enough he'd climb an eight-foot wire fence as soon as a three-foot iron one—and they had, too, as he knew they would.

That very first week he had come on the job, years and years ago, that young woman had jumped in the lake up there at the far end, near Ninety-sixth east. By the time they got to her with a boat and fished her out she was dead enough, poor gerl. And that man who had run out on the ice itself that bitter winter when the lake had frozen over except for a little open water hole where the old fountain pipe ran. Crazy, he must have been. He remembered how the man had just shoved himself down into that hole in the ice. He couldn't get to him in time, though he had shouted as he ran. A job it had been fishing him out that afternoon. Bitter work. What did they want to go and throw themselves in the pretty reservoir water for! Untidy and thoughtless. But then, you didn't think of such things when you were crazed with grief and that. When the boy Michael, his only son, had died, and when the Old Lady had got the stroke, and when Nell and Ed and the kids had come to the flat to live, why then he sometimes had thought that life wasn't much to go on with. But there always was the quiet and peace and responsibility of the Gatehouse to hold him up. . . .

He stopped thinking about that and went indoors. No good thinking of things like that now. He knocked the ash out of his pipe, carefully, into the big brass spittoon that Boyle had given him when that crazy Prohibition had come in and closed his place over on Columbus and Sixty-fifth.

Quarter to four. He had done everything there was to do. For the last time he had had his lunch in the little wooden enclosure that he liked to call his office, there in one corner of the big stone-walled room. He always brought his lunch with him, put up by Nell (not as good as the Old Lady's had been, though Nell said her way was more nourishing and healthy for him. Vitamins, God save us all!). He had brewed his cup of tea, strong and black the way he liked it in spite of the heat outdoors. It put new life into him. He had washed his dishes and made everything shipshape. He saw that all was in order—his report blanks, a pencil (he'd give that pencil to Noonan as a present, just to show there were no hard feelings).

He had polished the brass parts. He had rubbed the control board until it glittered. Then down in the operating chamber for a last look. For the first time the climb up the stairs seemed wearisome, endless. Fifty-eight, fifty-nine, sixty—sixty-one.

What could be keeping Noonan? They were like that nowadays. No sense of responsibility, not caring whether the job suffered or not. He had the right to go at four if he wanted to, Noonan or no Noonan, but he didn't want the nightman to show him the ropes. The last of it, but his job just the same, showing the new man around, explaining where this was and that, what time the calls came in, how the report should be made out. And to tell him never to leave the Gatehouse while on duty. Never. He remembered the one time he had left the place. His rule was not to step more than ten feet from the door to where the privet hedge grew, so that if the phone rang he could hear it. That one time when the girl had been thrown from her horse in the bridle path right there below the bridge facing the Gatehouse south door. He had run to pick her up as she lay there in the road, cut and bleeding so that her golden hair was dark and sticky. That minute the phone must have rung and kept on ringing and he hadn't heard it with all the hullabaloo and the girl lying there like death.

"Brophy! Where've you been?" The inspector's voice on the telephone, hard as nails. "I've been ringing for ten minutes straight, and more. Don't try to tell me you were down in the operating chamber." So then he had told him about the girl and how she looked like done for. The inspector had toned down a little then, but he'd barked just the same that the mounted police was there on the bridle path, it was his duty to attend to runaways and accidents on the beat.

"The cop wasn't there to see. I'm a man and a human being. Would I see a gerl stretched there in the road, white as death and the blood streaming from her head, and not help! I'll give you my job now if that's what's expected of me!" Dan always had been proud of the way he spoke up to the inspector that day.

Five minutes to four. He looked out through the folding metal gate at the south door, facing the bridge and the bridle path. A cruel, blistering day. Mothers with their babies in gocarts with wobbly wheels. They spread their bits of blanket on the parched grass beneath the trees and lay there through the long drowsy afternoon and got the good of the Park. They were the ones needed it, he reflected. The usual group of starched white-clad nursemaids were seated on the stone coping near the building itself, in the scant shade. Talking to their Park beaux, good-for-nothing bums most of them, meeting the nursegirls and coaxing small change out of them and pretending to be crazy about them, while the poor kids were left squalling or else running out into the bridle path, not being watched.

He never had let Michael when he was alive, or Nelly and her kids, come and play in or around the Gatehouse. It wasn't business. If they came to the Park they had to take what they could get of it like all the rest, and no favors, just because their pa and grampa was a Gatehouse tender. Engineer. Gatehouse Engineer.

Well! Two minutes to four. Four, you might say, and no Noonan. He turned back into the cool of the house. Guessed he'd call up the High Pressure Station down on Oliver Street. Noonan had been oiler at the High Pressure till he passed his stationary examination and got promoted to this. Oiler on one of the big engines. Great shining black-and-gold giants that reminded him for all the world of some people he had seen once in a circus—The Egyptian Queen's Eunuchs it was called—he didn't know how that one word was pronounced, but great black oily giants they had been, too, with gold on their wrists and arms and around their middles. Slaves.

There was a breeze between the two open doors, north and south. He loved the north door best. That great circle of water, blazing and still this July afternoon. There were winter days the wind whipped it up and made waves you'd think it was the ocean. Other times, like today, it was like a sheet of hot glass. In the winter the ice went shush-clink, shush-clink, like music. Staring at it now he tried to decide when he liked it best. Well sir, hard to say, and that's a fact. He stood. He glanced all around and up. Like a good-bye. On the wall over the lake-side doorway there was a plaque, bronze, with a lot of names on it. One stood out. FAIRCHILD, CONTRACTOR. 1858. He had built the stone house that had been Dan Brophy's castle these thirty-five years. And thanks to you, Mr. Fairchild sir.

"Hi, Pop!"

Dan whirled. Yes, there he was. Noonan. His big shoulders blocked the south doorway. He rattled the bars of the folding gate that was kept locked. He peered in facetiously, making a face like a prisoner behind bars, or an ape. Kids sometimes did that. It always made Dan mad.

"Oh, it's you, Noonan. I thought you wasn't coming, maybe you'd changed your mind about would you accept the job or not." There, he had said something he hadn't meant to. But Noonan wasn't put out.

"What's the hurry! I'll be cooped up here till I'm seventy, like you, and that's a good thirty-five years. Time enough to sit in this death house and get rheumatism, I'll say."

"I've got no rheumatism," Dan said. "I'm strong and hearty as ever I was."

"Sure, Grampa. You're a tough guy. How's for a scrap? Want to fight?" He doubled his fists and danced around Dan like a prizefighter.

"I bet I could give you a good scrap at that, for all you're so young and cocky."

"Save it for the girls, Pop. Look, where 'll I put my things?" He had brought a little bundle.

Dan became official. "Here." He led the way to the little office enclosure. "I'm all ready to go. I want to show you the ropes first so you'll get the hang of the place. Maybe we'd better start down below in the operating chamber, that's the important place."

"Oh, take it easy. I'll find my way around." He looked all about the bare cool gray room and glanced at the lake through the open north door. "That's the puddle, huh? Well, I guess after the High Pressure Station I can manage this one-horse machine."

Dan's face was set and stern. He went on, doggedly, "This here is the control board——"

"Okay, okay, Pop. I catch on."

"Look here, you think you're smart, but this place is important. It isn't what you're used to, Greasy Pants, with nothing to do but oil a black engine every so often, a child could do it. Stationary engineers in the Waterworks, we're important men and the running of the stations and resavoys and gates depends on us. It's us provides water for the kids to bathe, and for cooking and washing and drinking for millions and millions of folks in New York. Where 'd they be without us! You got to think of that when you take on a job like this, young feller me lad."

"Yeh, we're great little guys, all right. What's that? That shed thing in the corner?"

"That's my office—the office. You can make yourself a nice hot cup of tea in here, too, when the damp gets you, winters."

"Tea!" He roared with laughter.

Dan regarded him searchingly. "You're not a drinking man, I hope. Drink don't mix with this job, let me tell you."

"Oh, I take a drink now and then with the boys. But working I have a bottle of milk with my lunch."

"You'll find tea keeps you warmer."

"I don't need nothing to keep me warm. I'm a hot baby just the way I stand." He slapped his chest a resounding blow.

Just so he had felt thirty-five years ago, Dan reflected. Not such a big fella maybe, but strong and tough.

This is the east bay, this here is the west bay.

Noonan listened as an adult listens to a child's prattle; he seemed to be enjoying some private joke. He grinned as he listened and nodded his head. It was well after four now, and Quirk, the nightman, had come on. Dan introduced the two men, stiffly. He was going to do his duty to the end.

The telephone rang. There was something sharply insistent about its ring, as though the very tone of its bell divulged its emergency. Dan started toward it. Then he looked at Noonan, but Quirk answered it. His face then became an almost childlike study in surprise, unbelief, horror. He glanced at the control board. "Why, no sir. They're all okay. It must 've been something else—is it—you say it's on again now—well, nothing's happened here. . . . No, Brophy's off, you know, for good. . . . He's still here in the Gatehouse but he's leaving. . . . Oh no, he wouldn't do a thing like that. Not Dan. . . . Yessir, I'll call you back."

He leaped to the control board, examined it. All was in order.

"What's wrong?" Dan Brophy demanded. "What's that about me you said?"

"That was the Chief. Main office says they been swamped with calls the water in this section's been off for five good minutes."

Noonan began to laugh aloud now. Not so heartily, perhaps, as he had planned, but loudly enough, nevertheless, and the effect was aided by the way he slapped his own thighs. "The joke's on old Dan! I was just having a bit of fun when you turned your back and was explaining so solemn about this was the east and this was the west and this the north and that the south, why I just snapped her off for a minute, for a joke, see?"

The two men stared at him. "I'll have you fired," said Quirk.

"Not me, buddy. I got my papers."

Silent, Dan walked with dignity to the office and gathered up his things: his little spirit lamp, his cup and saucer, his pencil (let him get his own pencil now, the ape), his old sweater that Annie had knitted for him years ago, against the cold and damp, his rubbers for winter days down in the operating chamber.

He came out. His bundle under his arm he shook hands in silence with Quirk. He turned and looked at Noonan and the effect was that of a tall man looking down at an insect, though Noonan towered inches above him.

"It's you," Dan said very low, for there were people outside the open south door, in the shade, "it's you and your kind they call the younger generation is ruining the world. Nothing is sacred to you—jobs nor duty nor responsibility nor nothing. Joke, is it! It's jokers like you scum will bring the country to ruin and the world to an end. Mark me!"

"Aw, it was just in fun, Pop! Can't you take a joke?"

Dan Brophy unlocked the folding iron gate and stepped out into the withering July sunshine. The reservoir path stretched ahead of him, a last long mile.

"You're to keep the hedge clipped," he called over his shoulder to Noonan grinning in the doorway.

"Sure thing, Pop. I'll bite it off every morning after breakfast."

LOVE IN HARLEM

ALAN CAREER had eaten six of the hot delicate little soft-shell crabs, their white meat melting on the tongue. He had eaten the buttery sweet corn and crisp stacks of French-fried potatoes and a vast bowl of red raspberries iced and sugared. He had drunk his long cold drink with the mint stuck in the side of the glass. He hoped he wouldn't have a stomach-ache. You couldn't, he argued to himself, when you had enjoyed a meal as he had that one. The digestive juices or something took care of that. Instead of iced coffee Dahlia brought him a small cup of black hot. He felt soothed, rested, incredibly refreshed, and not at all lonely.

When he had found that the water mysteriously was not running, and after his irate protest to Bauers, the new superintendent, he had thrown himself on the bed a moment to cool off and wait for the water. And he had slept briefly, in spite of the heat. He had wakened feeling curiously free and light and happy. He was a little ashamed of the feeling with Patty and Susan hardly more than an hour out at sea. But he enjoyed the soaring sensation nevertheless. He had barely had time for his bath and a cigarette and a long cold drink before Dahlia had summoned him to dinner. And what a dinner!

So now he sat by the window with the electric fan going, feeling fine. He left the lamps unlighted. It was very early, and brilliant daylight. He heard Dahlia stirring about in the kitchen as though she were hurrying with the dishes. She wanted to get up to Harlem, that was it. Vaguely he wondered how she had the energy on a night like this. He thought idly of what he should do with his evening. It was nice to do nothing. Might go over to the newsreel, later. Air conditioned. But those damned war pictures, or travel films. The canals of Holland. He might just stroll over to that cool place by the pond in the Park at Seventy-second and sit there and breathe the fresh air. He heard Dahlia telephoning briefly, in a low voice with a certain timbre. Dahlia rarely telephoned. It was one of the things Patty liked about her.

Suddenly she appeared before him now, lounging there by the window, a transformed Dahlia. She was wearing a chocolate brown and white print, very smart, and a large brown hat. She had rouged her cheeks and her lips just a little and her eyes looked large and lustrous. She wore neat high-heeled pumps so that her badly articulated shanks seemed slim and almost shapely. Big-bosomed, trim, she looked handsome now.

"I just thought I'd let you know I'm going, Mr. Career."

"All right, Dahlia. That was a grand dinner you gave me."

"Well, those raspberries was awful high. Terrible. Seems they're scarce or something, it's the wet spring we had and then this heat all of a sudden, the man said. I had to go three places to get 'em, and high! Mis' Career would be wild." She giggled a little, nervously.

"That's all right. They were worth it. . . . How did you eat your dinner and get dressed so fast?"

"I didn't eat. I'm eating uptown."

Uptown. It was a term she always applied to Harlem, that mysterious city within a city. "A beau, eh? Good girl, Dahlia. Just so you're back for my breakfast."

She laughed lightly, evasively.

He took out his billfold, he held out a five-dollar bill. "All that extra work packing for Mrs. Career and Susan and Miss Mapes, and that running around in the heat on Lexington and that good dinner——"

"Mrs. Career gave me a dollar." She hesitated.

He was furious. He took out another five, recklessly, and put it in her mauve palm with the other. Her eyes widened. "Oh, Mr. Ca-reeah!"

She was off. He heard the bump and slam of the service elevator. He reflected that they knew nothing about her, really. She had lived in their apartment a daily and necessary part of their lives, and they knew nothing about her except that she was good and kind and honest and sympathetic; a gifted cook; and that she loved Susan. As if that weren't enough to know about anybody, he thought. When she came to them Patty had asked if she was married and she had said, no'm, she had been married, but not at present. Dahlia Thomas. Sometimes—rarely—she had telephone calls. They were brief, but her voice and manner changed. They took on another note, a fine informality. When she answered the telephone in a call from one of Patty's friends she was very correct.

"Mrs. Career's apartment. . . . Yes. . . . I'll see if she's in. . . . What's the name, please?" But in her own private talks, "Yeh? . . . Oh, hello, there! . . . Sure am! . . . Where was you last night?" A soft-throated giggle. She could speak correctly enough, but now she lapsed into an easy illiteracy as though dropping a stage role.

Five years in the house, he reflected, and they really knew nothing about her.

Dahlia got off the subway, came up the stairs at One Hundred and Thirty-fifth Street and emerged into the full light of Harlem's Lenox Avenue. It was almost eight o'clock and she hurried, stepping along with a free stride in spite of her stilted heels. Lenox was not yet blooming for the night. Harlem's work day was a long one. Its neon lights were not yet turned on, its music had not yet started. They had just begun to stream home to Harlem—the truck drivers, the seamstresses, the part-time maids, the girls who slept "out", the lavatory attendants, the dock hands, the switchboard operators, the elevator boys. They poured out of the L trains and subways to savory suppers and dark noisome rooms, to leisure and music and dancing and sleep. Housewives and returning workers scurried into the neighborhood pork and sausage and fish shops. From open windows, block on block, you smelled food in frying fat, you heard snatches of melody—a mouth harmonica, a banjo or guitar, a voice in song. Never unrhythmic, never unvital music.

Dahlia's quick light step carried her past the dozens of beauty parlors that dotted the region and she wished she had time to have her hair done fresh and clean and chick. The beauty-parlor window signs announced Croquignole Wave, 75c.

She had telephoned him to put on the stove, in water, the chunk of fat pork that was in the icebox but she couldn't be sure that he had done it. He had no head for things like that, and why should he? Maybe he hadn't even stayed home. You never knew whether he would stay or go. That was part of the thrill of it.

She came to the row of strangely blackened houses, once good middle-class brownstone fronts, on One Hundred and Thirty-seventh just off Lenox. Up the stairs, one flight, two, three, four, quickly, quickly. She could smell the pork bubbling. Cooking too fast. She'd fix all that. Wouldn't it be like him wanting pork and cabbage a night like this! As she put the key in the door she heard the sound of the piano, one phrase over and over again. Her heart beat fast.

There he was at the piano, sitting half turned away from it in the grotesque position he always assumed during the long hours when he sat there composing. His lean flexible legs crossed at the knees and sort of twined around each other, yet his feet managing to reach the pedals; his long fingers seeming to flow over the keys like chocolate sauce on vanilla ice cream. He was in his sleeveless white undershirt and a pair of wrinkled white linen pants. He glanced up as she came in but his face remained immobile. Only his eyes changed a little, grew wider then half closed again as before. He went on playing, his head jerking in time to the music, one great flat foot in its sockless bedroom slipper beating out the rhythm with a gentle slap-slap. From the top of the smudged and scarred piano his clarinet grinned at him with all its teeth.

She had stopped at the grocer's and now she dumped her bundles on the kitchen table, crossed to him at the piano, bent over him. She kissed the back of his long lean bare neck as a mother kisses a child. He went on playing. His face and head might have been used as a portrait of the tragedy of his race—the tortured eyes, the lines of dignity and submission, the pouting childlike mouth, the amazing flash of white teeth so unexpectedly brilliant like a lightning flash in the somber cloud of his mask. She looked at him, he looked up at her from the piano stool, he nodded and smiled and went on with his music. She was quick, lively, capable; he was slow moving, slow talking, dreamy. You couldn't tell, half the time, whether he had heard what you said. He was thinking of something else. His music, usually. A tune running through his head. He had made up dozens of them. She never ceased to marvel at the wonder of it. "Listen at this," he said now, playing.

She listened, her head cocked carefully to one side. She knew little about music. She had only the unerring rhythm sense of her race.

"Listen at this," he said again, like a man in his sleep.

It was a complicated thing, yet slyly simple, too. "It's grand," Dahlia said. "It's just wonderful, Lacy. It's hot licks, that's what."

She always said that. He repeated patiently like a child who is tugging at his mother's skirts, wanting attention, "No, but listen at this, Dahlia."

"Um-hmm, Lacy." She went into the bedroom and peeled off her smart print dress and her pink slip and corset and came back in her all-over work dress that buttoned right down the front, neat and fresh. There were only two rooms: the kitchen-sitting room where the piano and the stove mingled affably, and the dark stifling bedroom with its double bed. She went to the stove now, lifted the cover off the pot, clapped it back on and brought the kettle to the sink. There she poured off the salt water and covered the meat with fresh. She put it back on the stove and began to cut a head of cabbage into the simmering pot.

She was ten years older than he. Sometimes she was frightened by her own luck. It couldn't last. Here she was, thirty-six, and Lacy only twenty-six. She was only working out and he was Lacy Bigger playing piano and clarinet, both, in the Jungle Ballroom with Chick Trueblood's Famous Rhythm Orchestra. White and black swarmed up there every night enchanted, held, hypnotized by the perfection of the swing music that issued from that group of music-bewitched Negroes. All over Harlem they knew and applauded Lacy when he played a clarinet or piano solo or when they announced one of his own original compositions. And he stayed with her. He let her pay for this flat, for the installments on the piano. Let her cook his dinners on her days off. Curiously enough, though he loved fine clothes he would not let her pay for those. On Sunday afternoon in the Lenox Avenue style parade or on St. Nicholas Avenue in the late autumn or the first spring days when the Harlem bucks were out in their new finery —French blue topcoats, postilion style, pockets dashingly slashed, patent-leather shoes, pearl gray fedoras, bright yellow walking sticks, pink or blue shirt—Lacy appeared a somber figure, but never drab. In his dark brown or navy blue or black he had an effortless grace and even distinction.

As Dahlia set the table for supper she chatted through the music. If he heard he gave no sign. "She left today. My, they looked swell! Susan was like a rose. Blue, one of her handmade French, and a coat and hat to match though it was too hot for the coat but you know how Miz Career is—Susan had to look traveling correct, like her ma. She gave me a dollar when she left and said take good care of him, as if I wouldn't anyway. And he up and gave me ten, I thought I'd bust, you could of knocked me down with a breath. It 'll pay the piano installment and part the rent money. I made him a mess of soft-shell crabs he said it was the best dinner he ever eat. He's a sweet fella, that's what he is." She laughed fondly. Then, as an after-thought, "She don't rightly understand him."

"Listen at this, Dal," said Lacy patiently. He played the air again, just a few bars, listening intently as though to something far away and elusive.

"Mm-hmm, Lacy. It's wonderful. It's the best yet." Just to be near him was enough, to know that he was here in the flat, playing, this wonder boy Lacy Bigger.

Lazy Begger they called him at the Jungle, but she knew different. She knew he was working all the time in his mind. He never stopped working. Tunes ran through his head by day, by night.

"Hongry?"

"H'm?"

"I says, hongry?"

"Not much. Had me hamn-eggs for breakfast, big saucer huckleberries and cream and some hot bread."

"My land, what time, Lacy! What time you have all that?"

"Usual time. 'Bout three."

"But when I phoned asked you what you'd like for supper you said fat meat and cabbage. If you ain't hongry."

He did not answer. She went on with her preparations for dinner. She seasoned the contents of the pot —a handful of fresh celery tops to give delicacy of flavor; pepper, a pinch of kitchen bouquet. The cabbage was simmering with the meat in a pool of golden fat. She went into the other room and stripped the tumbled bed, replacing the rumpled sheets with fresh ones, sheathed the pillows in neatly laundered cases.

Over all she spread the rose taffeta cover that Mrs. Career had given her when she changed her bedroom color scheme. "In case you ever get married again," she had said laughingly. "Though heaven forbid."

Dahlia dusted the bedroom and wiped up the floor with a mop. Artlessly she shook the small matting rug out of the window and laid it again. Her face was wet with the heat and exertion. Now and then she peered into the bubbling kettle. Lacy continued to play. He would play one bar over and over a score of times, a hundred times, his eyes glazed. A cigarette dangled from his lips, cold. Sometimes he made little marks on a piece of paper propped up on the music holder.

"Wonder is it too hot for light biscuits I'd have to use the oven but they'd go good with the pork gravy. But maybe it's too hot with you at the piano, so near."

"Biscuits would go good," Lacy said almost a full minute later, as though the words had just penetrated his consciousness. "I ain't hot."

It was as though he had given her an accolade. Swiftly she got out the mixing bowl, spoon, flour, baking powder. She beat and stirred and rolled and cut. She had worked since six that morning, packing for Mrs. Career, cleaning the apartment after the travelers' departure, cooking Alan Career's dinner. Yet all her movements were brisk and sure and full of vitality. Now and then she glanced at him as a work-driven mother throws a reassuring glance at a child playing in the room. He went on with his repetitious strumming.

"Bring an evening paper with you?"

"Oh, Lacy, I forgot! I was in such a tear to get here I forgot."

He said nothing. He went on with his music. She slid the pan of biscuits into the oven, looked down at herself worriedly, brushed the flour off her skirt, then with a little shrug as though, after all, nothing mattered but Lacy, she opened the door and ran down the four flights of steps to the street, just as she was. In less than five minutes she was back, the illustrated tabloid in her hand. She held it out to him. With a flicker of his eyelids he indicated that she was to put it on the piano top.

They sat down to supper at quarter of ten. The room was stifling. She heaped his plate with cabbage and the slices of pork, ruddy and gold; with biscuits and cream gravy. She ate a little but he, after a mouthful or two, ate nothing. He smoked cigarette after cigarette. They talked little. Her glance lingered anxiously on his face. She did not ask if the food suited him, or if he was not hungry, or why he did not eat. She knew that, for the time, she did not exist for him, the food did not exist, that only music marched in his brain. The hot heavy victuals lay on his plate, almost untouched.

She brought out the vast slice of chilled watermelon that she had carried with her when she first came in. He looked at it as at a strange object. She had seen him distrait before, but never like this. Her patient adoring eyes searched his face. His cheeks seemed hollower than when she came in, his eyes were dull and leaden, the cigarette dangled limp from a corner of his mouth. He sat, staring into space. Sometimes his head waggled jerkily in time to some ghostly unheard tune.

Suddenly his face kindled. The transformation was frightening. His eyeballs seemed ready to start from their sockets, the muscles around his jaw worked, the veins stood out on his temples. He shoved his plate away so roughly that the gravy slopped on the clean cloth she had spread. He reached the piano in two strides of his long legs, his slippers slapping after him, he melted to the piano stool, he seemed to take the battered instrument into his long arms. He began to play now, not uncertainly, not querulously as he had before but masterfully; triumphantly.

"Listen at this!" he shouted above the paean. "Listen at this!"

She sat there. Then she rose; she seemed pulled to her feet by the compelling rhythm. She stood a moment as if listening, then she began to dance alone, trucking at first, then her steps became more and more intricate, her movements took on a barbaric frenzy. Faster and faster he played. Her body writhed and twisted and whirled to keep pace with it. "Listen at this!" he yelled. "Boy! Listen at this!" Exultation in his voice.

He stopped at last. She dropped, dripping and exhausted, into her chair. Now the sweat was dripping, too, from his hands and face that had been so clammy. He got up from the piano and went over to the sink and sluiced his head and arms and mopped them, grinning. He came over to her and kissed her, roughly, and ran his hands over her. He sat down at the table and began to eat, voraciously.

"Honey boy, don't eat that! It's all cold. Let me get you a plate of fresh from the stove."

"It's grand." His mouth was full and running over. He stabbed great forkfuls of the dripping pork and cabbage, wolfing them down. He sloshed halves of biscuit around in the gravy. "That's the tune I been rassling with since way back last spring and couldn't make it come right no way. Good hot July weather and it clears my head makes me feel good. What 'll I call it? Hot July. How's that for name? Hot July. You wait. You see. They'll be playing it dance music all next autumn and winter, every band in Harlem 'll be playing it—Harlem, hell! Every band in New York! Benny Goodman 'll be playing it, and Duchin and all of 'em, and Whiteman. You wait. You see. Je's, I feel like I'd come out of a fever. Leave me have a glass of beer, will you, honey?"

She hesitated, then fetched it and poured him a scant glass. "You know you never drink before you work, sugar. Eat slower. You'll make yourself sick, hot night like this."

"I ain't hot. I feel fine."

It was almost eleven. He got up, lighted a cigarette, took a long drag at it, then stretched his arms high above his head and kicked his legs out, first one and then the other, as though he were trying to get the stiffness out of them after a long sleep.

As she cleared the supper things she heard him dressing in the bedroom. Presently he came out and began to pack his clarinet and his music. He had on his smart white coat and his black pants with the broad satin stripe up the side, and his patent-leather pumps and the romantic black cummerbund wound around his slim flat waist. She came over and straightened his black tie, though it did not need straightening. He held out his hand and she put five dollars into it. She put up her face; he bent and kissed her.

"We got to rehearse. I want they should play this tonight. They got to get it right for tonight." He was talking, not to her but to himself. He lighted another cigarette and was out of the room; she heard his feet incredibly swift and light on the stairs.

Neatly she put the remaining food into the refrigerator, she made the room tidy. She washed his socks and handkerchiefs and underwear and hung them to dry. In the bedroom she turned back the spread and lay down to rest briefly and she groaned with weariness as her body sank down in the breathless little room. She slept half an hour. Awake, she washed her body at the bowl and patted herself with pungent toilet water and powder and felt refreshed. By the time she had dressed again carefully and made up it was well after midnight.

She tucked a five-dollar bill—her second—into an old envelope, placed the envelope on the piano keys where his eye must fall on it first thing tomorrow, and closed down the piano lid. She looked all about her. The flat was neat and clean. She turned off the light, shut the door after herself and locked it. The streets were brilliant and alive, the sidewalks were thronged as for a festival. Shuffling feet, music, gay rich caressing voices, girls in brilliant red and green and yellow and pink. Violent color, violent sound, carnival spirit. But she hurried along, no part of it with her serious gentle face and her quiet brown print.

At the Jungle Ballroom they knew her well, she went to her little corner table near the orchestra platform almost hidden by the artificial palms. She sat demurely at the table and ordered her small glass of light beer from Stompy Sam, the waiter.

There he was at the piano, her Lacy boy. His clarinet lay on top of it. The orchestra was playing *Swingin' Earth* and the floor was crowded with white people and black, men and women. The vast room was artificially cooled. The music stopped, there was perfunctory applause, the dancers drifted to their tables and booths. She leaned forward, Lacy swung round on the piano stool, his eyes sought her corner and his eyelids just flickered. That was all, but it was enough. She leaned back, satisfied.

That little Fredi Buzzell the blues singer slithered out from behind the palms to do her number. The roll of the drum. They threw the spot on her in the center of the bare floor in her tight white satin that was only a skirt and a shield over her breasts, a scarlet chiffon handkerchief dripping like blood from her hand. She sang and wriggled. Nothing extra and never was, Dahlia thought. Only her figgah, you had to hand it to her there. Dahlia looked down at herself and sighed a little.

Fredi Buzzell gave a last screech, a final wiggle and a wave of the scarlet handkerchief and was gone to fair applause. Hundreds as good as Fredi in Harlem, and better, Dahlia knew. Sex appeal, probably, like that Josephine Baker, she couldn't sing or dance or anything but they say dukes and lords go for her in Paris and Europe.

An interval, then Chick Trueblood, the orchestra leader, stood up and raised his right hand. There was a ruffle of the drums. Her eyes went to Lacy seated there at the piano, his hands listless on his knees, his face dreamy, remote.

"La-dees an' gen-tel-men! This evenin' I have the honor to announce that Chick Trueblood's orchestra —yes'm, that's me, thank you—will now endeavor to present for the first time in this or any other country an original numbah by one of our own members of our own celebrated orchestra. The numbah entitled *Hot July* is composed and arranged entirely and especially for this orchestra and played here and now for the first time by Mr. Lacy Bigger. . . . Stand up, Lacy, let the girls see you and let the folks all give you a great big hand. MISTAH LACY BIGGAH!"

Lacy looked around, still seated. Then, inch by inch, he uncoiled his long lean body and stood a moment, drooping, his head averted from the perfunctory applause.

"You wait," Dahlia said aloud, fiercely, though no one heard her but Stompy Sam. "Just you wait!"

Lacy melted fluidly into his chair again. He struck the opening chord of *Hot July* and the orchestra swung into it with him. They were to play it all next winter, and the winter after that and after that, though they didn't know it then. It was to be incorporated into the music language of America; and orchestras in Cairo and Paris and Venice and Budapest and London were to play it, wherever people gathered to dance; and it was to be played at Carnegie Hall by the Symphony Orchestra, and the red plush boxes were to shout bravos at the lank limp black man who so lackadaisically came out to take his bow.

The floor had been crowded before; now it was a maelstrom. They were not merely dancing couples, they danced, seemingly, like a ballet, moved by one emotion, swayed by a common rhythm. It was like Prince Igor, like Petrouschka, like Scheherazade in color, movement, frenzy, that crowd.

When it was finished they stood a split second. Then they began to stamp and shout and smack their hands together sharply. There was nothing forced about this. This was the real thing.

Dahlia was looking at him. Her eyes were enormous, they seemed to glow as though a lamp were lighted somewhere behind them. Her bosom rose and fell as though she had been running.

Suddenly, out of the mob, a little figure that had been dancing with the rest darted free and leaped to the orchestra platform. It was a white satin figure, slim and lithe, with a scarlet handkerchief streaming after it like a banner. Like a cat she gained the platform, screamed shrilly, sprang high and hung herself about the standing Lacy's limp frame, her thin brown arms about his lean neck, her bare legs with the scarlet satin-shod feet locked about his legs. So she hung for a moment, a she-panther on its prey.

Dahlia Thomas stood up. The knuckles of her black hand gleamed white where she clutched the chair, her lips drew back from her teeth in a snarl, the room reeled and swayed before her eyes, she started forward.

But Lacy's strong wiry hand reached up then and

unclasped the brown arms from about his neck; gently, yet with power and firmness and a terrible deliberation, he turned the little figure over and slapped her soundly, just once, on her white satin bottom. Then, still gently, he tossed her onto the unused bass drum where she landed with a conclusive boom. "Scat!" Lacy said lazily.

The crowd howled. Shaking, Dahlia sank back into her chair. Her eyes were on him. Unsmiling he sleepily raised his palm to her—just a barely perceptible gesture—the opening of the palm, a little jerk at the top of it as the hand came up. That was all.

"Another beer, Miz' Thomas?" said Stompy Sam.

She shook her head. Blindly she paid for her beer. She felt she must choke with happiness if she did not get out. Out into the air she walked a few blocks, but then her feet began to hurt in the high heels. She had scarcely sat down these past twenty hours. She sank into the subway seat but she was not conscious of weariness. She was not conscious of anything. Happy. That was all. She let herself into the Career back entrance and flicked on the kitchen light. A saucer and a spoon in the sink. He had had a little snack. She washed the plate and spoon and put them in their place. She wound her alarm clock, yawning fearfully so that all her strong white teeth showed against the red mouth. Two o'clock, and after. She was beat, she told herself. Dead on her feet. She rolled into her narrow bed in the stifling back room with the hot-water pipes running through it and she slept, and as she slept there was a half smile on her gentle good face.

DANCING IN THE PARK

IT WAS SURPRISINGLY COOL in the center of the Park, there by the pond near Seventy-second Street. Alan Careeer sat on a bench looking over the water. It was actually cool enough for a pipe. It putt-putted peacefully as he sat there. The place was almost deserted. People didn't know about it much, hidden there in a sort of hollow among the trees. Some small boys were playing near the edge of the pool in the fading light. There was a splash, and another. Two of them had jumped in and were swimming in the shallow water while the others kept a sharp watch out for the cop. Bathing was forbidden in this pond. Boys sailed their toy boats in it, and grown men, too, frequently. Once or twice Alan Career had strolled over here on Sunday morning and he had seen men his own age, and older, absorbed in the maneuvers of tiny ships they themselves had fashioned—exquisite miniatures of the yacht builders' craft. Carefully they placed their boats in the pond, these nautical men who were moored to the land, and they fed their starved urge for the sea and the salt breeze by bending all morning over the stone parapet watching the little land breeze fill the sails of their beloved boat, fancying themselves actually aboard a slim beauty like this, with a line like a scimitar, and a hundred times its size.

He had never been here before at this time of day. Patty wasn't one to come out to the Park of an evening, like a servant girl.

The young ragamuffins were coming out now with hoarse triumphant shouts, having bested the law, and were dressing in the near-by bushes. It was almost dark. A grateful freshness seemed to emanate from the trees, the grass, the water.

I'm sitting here, he thought, like an old married man, the kind you used to see in the funny papers before the *New Yorker* and *Esquire*. What was that song? *My Wife's Gone to the Country, Hurray! Hurray!* I guess they don't have jokes about summer widowers in *Esquire*. They've gone out of fashion. Fashion. I'm fashionable. Hell, yes! Me and my wife, both. Alan Career photographed at El Morocco with his lovely young wife, the former Patty Mallett. . . .

Chillicothe, Ohio. Local boy makes good in New York. Good and lousy. Had to have her mother take her to Europe, like a damned failure.

There came to his ears the sound of music. Some fools in the Park with a radio; or maybe just a radio taxi waiting for a fare along a Fifth Avenue side street. No, it was a real band playing hard. Must be one of those band concerts they had over near the Mall somewhere. But it didn't sound like anything as conventional as a band concert. It had the insistent rhythm of swing. He rose after a minute or two and strolled in the direction of the music.

There was the bleat of the saxophone, the beat of the drum, the pipe of the cornet, the blare of brass.

Vaguely he remembered that there was some sort of municipal park dance in the summer. Keep the kids off the streets, or on 'em, he didn't know which. He was not prepared for what he now saw as he turned off the walk, crossed the wide roadway and came upon the vast space in front of the bandstand.

Thousands of them. Thousands and thousands of boys and girls—eighteen, twenty, twenty-five—dancing on the cement in the open air. The arc lights cast a golden glow upon them. As he came to the outer edge of the watchers that encircled the dancing floor the music stopped with a final blare and the dancers swarmed off the floor. They brushed past him, they jostled him, they made for the shadowy spaces that lay so invitingly beyond the dance floor. Hatless, all of them. The boys were the kind he saw in shipping rooms, at minor desks, standing behind chain-store grocery counters, delivering packages, driving bundle vans—working for twenty or twenty-five dollars a week. They had on clean blue shirts, their hair was slicked back, they had a pleasant city sunburn. They wore suit coats. One or two even sported white coats smartly pinched in at the waist.

The girls were in summer prints and little wash frocks and organdies. Thin stuff, and transparent for the most part. They wore their hair as Patty wore hers, he noticed—simple and cut rather long so that it curled where the ends just touched their shoulders. Their hair looked as if it had just been washed. It sprang alive and shining. The style was flattering and made a frame for their faces so that they seemed very young and wide-eyed.

Almost immediately the band struck up. They played *Whoa Babe*. A second before the floor had been a deserted gray expanse. That first alert couple darted across the immense space like a pair of swallows in flight. Then the thousands swarmed upon it. Not an inch was left bare. Alan Career found himself grinning as he knocked the ash out of his pipe and edged his way to the rim of the dance floor, the better to see this exhilarating sight.

They danced in the curious style of the day and age. They jerked and twirled in the intricate St. Vitus steps of the Lindy Hop. Then, quite simply, they withdrew a little, and, arms about each other's waists, they ambled lackadaisically for all the world like young calves in a meadow. Suddenly the youth would catch the girl to him and twirl her in a breath-taking spin that made the onlooker's head whirl. They then kicked up their legs, swooped, dipped, jounced, and glided. As Alan Career watched their childlike antics he felt suddenly old and out of it. They were so young, so lacking in self-consciousness. Any boy, he noticed, would approach the lady of his choice and say, "Would you like to dance?" Very self-possessed, like a Yale blood at a Christmas dance at Pierre's. Usually the girl would nod her head, wordlessly. They were off. He was surprised to see that the girls, for the most part, wore rather sturdy shoes with heavy soles and sensible heels. Coquettish footgear seemed to be the exception. The boys had their trousers well turned up at the cuff so that you saw their lively shanks as they capered. He thought that some of them must have danced together for months, so expert were they, so intuitive each with the other's signals. Miles of practice must have been covered to perfect this amazing routine. Some of their steps were as intricate and exquisitely planned as those of a pair of professional entertainers at the Rainbow Room or the Waldorf. Yet there were others who had met at that moment and never before. An introduction evidently was not necessary. The music was their chaperon. Then Alan Career saw that this was not quite true, for here and there on the dance floor and at the fringe of the crowd were stern-faced and somewhat weary-looking women in khaki skirts and blouses and little military-looking caps. They kept an alert eye on the dancers and when a couple showed signs of too much energy even for that lively gathering, or too much emotion for the Park proprieties, they stepped quickly forward and tapped the offending pair on the shoulders.

Amused, he edged his way over to one of these rather formidable and martial figures.

"Uh—many dances like this?"

The observant eyes looked up at him and at what they saw, melted. "Every Tuesday and Thursday night. All over town."

"Great thing," he remarked, conversationally. "I wouldn't mind having a whirl myself." Then, aghast at the thought that she might consider this an invitation, "That is—uh—makes a fellow feel young again —you know."

But he need have had no fear. She had moved away, her basilisk eye sweeping the dance floor. He felt like a schoolboy who had talked out of turn to teacher. The music stopped again. Again they swarmed off the dance floor. They gathered into little groups, they stormed the ice-cream cone wagon, they indulged in heavy-handed banter, they shoved; there was a good deal of horseplay, heavy coquetry; and girlless boys marching lock step through the crowd, followed by scuffling and unconvincing shrieks.

"Stop it! Stop your shoving!"

"Look, Myrna's sore!" They pronounced it Moyna's so-ah.

"Whyn't you daincing?"

"I wouldn't daince with a stick like you, not if I was to staind here all night."

Or two boys huddled in dark conference. "I seen a couple of nice ones together but you was hoofing with that rock you picked up."

"Well, she looked okay. How would I know she was paralyzed from the hips down?"

The music struck up. That new song. They were rhyming ring time with swing time instead of with springtime as they used to when he was a kid back in Chillicothe, Ohio. There was a kind of cult of this new-old jazz among the boys and girls Alan remembered having heard. They worshipped it, the old gods having been destroyed, and having nothing better upon which to lavish their bewildered undirected young devotion. As they sped forth now at its summons they were magically transformed from the rather vulgar and commonplace giggling girls and oafish boys of a moment before into lovely pixies, fauns and sprites, free, graceful, uninhibited, disporting themselves in this urban concrete grove.

Alan Career's feet were tapping in time with the infectious rhythm. Someone brushed softly but unmistakably against the sleeve of his tweed coat. He looked down. A girl's voice said, "Oh, pardon!" He thought, well my gosh, I'm being picked up in the Park like a grocery boy. She was a funny-looking little thing, not pretty.

"Oh, hello!"

She looked a little disdainful. "Hello—if you want to start that way."

Well!

She nodded toward the madly whirling crowd on the dance floor. "Isn't this delicious!" in an affected little tone.

In the second glance, encompassed in a moment, he decided that, though the average boy in this mob would have passed her by in favor of one of the more obvious golden-haired sprites, she had a kind of charm. The word piquant came to his mind. She wore a gray dress that had a sort of ruching edging the square-cut neckline, rather low. Tight in the bodice, full in the skirt. Patty had one something like it. She had told him it was a dirndl, copied from the Austrian peasant girls' dresses. This particular little ersatz Austrian peasant had a wide red mouth, made wider and redder purposely, rather protuberant blue eyes, a nose that was too short. She was a good deal like a Pekingese. She looked up at him under her lashes as though she had been practicing looking up under her lashes. Not very good at it yet.

"My name's—uh—Alan. And you—? as they say in the novels."

"I'm Miss Lonely Heart like you read about in the papers."

This was going to be all right.

"Dance?"

She nodded. They danced. The floor was very unyielding and not smooth. It had been waxed with a soapy preparation. He knew now why the girls wore practical shoes and the boys turned up their trousers. She danced effortlessly and rhythmically. Her body was pliant and slim. She was little and light and it was pleasant. Patty was a tall girl, tennis and swimming, biggish bones and a lot of expert dieting to keep the thirty-four, with her shoulders. Miss Lonely Heart did not talk as she danced. At first he led her in the conventional steps to which he was accustomed. But little by little, and almost without his noticing it, she was guiding him into the steps in use by those about them. They essayed some of the convolutions he had watched from the sidelines. Not so bad. They whirled. Then, arms about each other's waists, they strolled. He felt young, foolish, irresponsible, and rather happy. He was sorry when the dance was finished. Hot, though.

"How about an ice-cream cone?"

She shuddered. Oh, no.

He was puzzled. He couldn't for the life of him

make out whether she was a nice girl trying to be not too common, or a not too common girl trying to be refined. That was it. Refinement. Terrible word.

"What is a young and lovely and fashionable gal like you doing in New York on a night like this?" He was rather proud of that lead in. Slick.

"It's no hotter than Long Island or Connecticut."

(You don't say.) "Is that where you'd be if you weren't here?"

"Maybe. Where would you be?"

(No dice.) "I like it fine right where I am. I'd rather be here this minute than any place in the world." (Phew!)

She turned on him another of those under-eyelash looks. Where had he seen that kind of eyework before? The movies, that was it. Pictures.

The music again. "Dance?"

She pointed to his fawn flannel trousers, very smart. "You'd better turn those up. They'll be ruined." Nice little thing. Practical for a kid. He began to feel rather paternal about her and wished he wouldn't. He turned up his trouser cuffs, displaying an alarming pattern of fawn and gray and scarlet plaid English socks which Patty had given him for Christmas.

Out on the floor they skimmed again. He felt expert and confident now. "Hi, Hot Socks!" yelled a demon lad from the sidelines. "Hot Socks!" his gang echoed with gusto. Alan didn't care at all. He kicked up his heels. They skimmed, dived, swooped, pranced, strolled, whirled. She was a feather in his arms, he swung her with one arm as he remembered having seen that Argentine fellow swing his partner at the Plaza Persian room. Almost at once one of the khaki basilisks touched him on the shoulder. "Sorry. We don't permit that."

Oh, very well. We've got plenty of other elegant steps and try and stop us. He smiled down at her, she smiled up at him (eyelash business). He held her a little closer. Her face became serious, dreamy. They were all serious, he noticed. He had remarked that from the first. They were lively but unsmiling. They did not talk, they did not laugh. They were enjoying themselves but it was a surface gaiety with an air of routine about it. From somewhere in the back of his head there popped a line from a play that he and Patty had seen. He hadn't liked the play much. Ibsen. *A Doll's House*. Thorvald, stricken at his wife's leaving, had cried to her, "But haven't you been happy?" And she had replied, sadly, "Not happy. Only merry."

That was what these youngsters were, dancing. Not happy. Only merry. Only merry. He must have said it aloud, unconsciously, for she looked up sharply. "What's that?"

Rather shamefacedly he explained, "I was just reminded of a line in a play. You young people today. Not happy—only merry."

Evidently she had never heard of it, wasn't interested, didn't understand. "I suppose you think you're a hundred."

"I'm thirty-four," he said gravely.

"I hate kids."

"You're a sweet thing."

They danced cheek to cheek. Her skin was fresh and smooth and resilient. If he had turned his head just half an inch he could have kissed her. He said so.

"Yes, and get put off the floor for good." Sharply.

"They can't see everything."

"Yes they can—those old drizzle-pusses."

"When are you going to break down and tell me all about yourself?"

But she was evasive. There was something guarded, calculated about her. "You're not one of those girl reporters, are you? Sent out to get a feature story on New York in the summertime, and I'll read all my brilliant cracks in next Sunday's tabloid?"

"Don't you wisht you knew."

"Wish."

"Pardon?"

"Wish, not wisht. And don't say pardon all the time like that. Who do you think you're fooling! Stop pretending and be yourself. Your own little darling self. Come on, before I get rough. Where do you live and who are you?"

"You married?"

"Yep."

"All the nice ones are married."

She was cute but hardly original, he thought. "Now I've told you, you tell——"

The band struck up *Home, Sweet Home.*

They danced wordlessly then, very close, and when the music ended he stood holding her in his arms for a moment because he wanted to, and she wanted him to, and all the others were doing the same, and the drizzle-pusses couldn't chase them off the floor now when they had to go, anyway.

The boys and girls were drifting off the floor and into the Park shadows. There was a dreamlike quality about their going. Back to the stuffy flats, the nagging harassed parents, the squalling brothers and sisters, the roar of the L trains outside their bedroom windows, the heat, tomorrow's job.

The cops, their smart coupés lined up at the roadside, were watching sharply. Outta the Park, boys and girls. Kindly but no nonsense about them. Outta the Park and home with you.

"Well," said dirndl, "good night. It's been—I mean I've had a swell time."

"Okay pleased to 've metcha hope we meet again sometime sister. There. How's that? Now let's stop pretending. It's too hot. Where do you want to go for a drink?"

"A drink?"

"Yes. You know—wet libation in a glass, preferably alcoholic."

"Oh, I don't think I——" Looking up at him, very little and gray and gold and wide-eyed.

"Cut it, won't you! A joke's a joke. Do you want to go downtown? Or how about the Carlyle bar just over on Madison? Or Longchamps? It's air-cooled."

"Well," she agreed reluctantly. "Only for a minute, though. You wouldn't ply a girl with liquor, would you?"

He hustled her into a taxi at Fifth. "Vulgar little baggage, aren't you? Is that the right answer? Now you've given a very fine performance. Very. Stop it! . . . No, not you, driver. I was talking to—— Go to Longchamps, will you, Madison and Seventy-eighth."

She giggled. "Oh, sir!"

He shook her then, not seriously, but as one who is exasperated. She slapped him. He kissed her hard. She screamed. The taxi stopped before Longchamps' lime-and-raspberry colored front.

"Well, that's over," Alan said. "Now we can be comfortable." And gave the driver a dollar on a twenty-five-cent ride for which the driver did not thank him, being a true New York taxi driver. For a moment he thought she actually was going to leave him. She started south on Madison, just a step, but he grasped her arm firmly and held her before him in the same compartment as they went through the revolving door.

"What will you drink? And wouldn't you like something to eat, after all that dancing?"

He didn't feel like eating; but a long cold drink! He was suddenly tired. Rye highball. Or a brandy and soda. No. Keep him awake.

"I'll have an Alexander cocktail."

He was aghast. "Oh, listen, you don't want that sickish sweet stuff this time of night."

"I do so!"

"All right." He was a little bored with it. "Only when you wake up with that oopsy feeling at 3 A.M. remember Papa warned you. Look, where do you live?"

"Over on Park—near Park, I mean."

"Make up your mind. Anyway, Park Avenue's a long street with lots of little streets cutting into it. I'll tell you what. I'll tell you all. I'm married. My wife's in Europe. I think you're sweet. I——"

"What's your job? I mean, where are you employed?"

"Ma'am, I ain't employed. I employ myself when I can get any business, which they say it's picking up and the Depression's over but they'll have to show me. I'm a desk worker. How's that? I work over a desk, a handsome desk, I'll admit, with a view and a secretary and push buttons and telephones and an office boy. But a wage slave just the same. And now won't you be honest and cozy, and I wish to God you wouldn't crook your little finger like that when you drink. You're not fooling me, you know. Not any more."

"I don't know what you mean."

"All right, all right. You're a bitter ender, I can see that."

She bridled. "I think it's about time you apologized for kissing me in the taxi like that, if you're a gentleman."

"I'm no gentleman, but how about that sock in the jaw you gave me? I suppose that's being a lady, eh?"

"Don't you talk——"

"Girl, you're as good as apologized to. One more drink and I'm down on my knees though Grampa's knees feel a little wore down after all that cavorting. Now then. Where do *you* work? Junior League?"

She threw him a sharp glance. "What makes you think I work anywhere?"

"I'm going to kiss you again when I take you home."

"You ain't—you're not going to take me home."

"You never were more mistaken in your life."

She was up, she was through the revolving door and down the street. His astounded gaze saw the elfin figure flash past the big plate-glass window, headed south. One shocked second and he, too, was on his feet, he was dashing after her. The head waiter, suave but firm, blocked him at the door. "Pardon me, sir. You are forgetting your check."

Alan Career fished in his pockets, he opened his bill-fold, there was nothing smaller than a ten-dollar bill. You couldn't, after all. Habit was too strong. He clutched his change after what seemed like hours, and whirled through the revolving door so that it spun like an electric fan after him. The kid was crazy. Cute but crazy. Out on the sidewalk he looked up the street as he ran. He could just discern her tiny figure tinier still in the Madison Avenue distance.

He had been a good runner in the Chillicothe high school track meets and at Dartmouth. But as he ran the caution of the past ten years of conventional New York training tugged at his coattails and told him he should not be doing this. The little dim gray figure darted round a corner and vanished. He made the corner in what would have been record-breaking time even in his Dartmouth days and it turned out to be his corner, his street. He could just see her. She was not running now. Poor little kid. Heh, wait a minute Alan my boy. You can't be seen chasing a girl down the street at one o'clock in the morning. The cops have a word for it. You'd look nice in nine o'clock police court, up for molesting women on the street. Patty 'd like that in the Paris *Herald*. He glanced over his shoulder to see if he was being watched, and when he faced forward again she had vanished completely. He stopped running then and was conscious that the sweat was streaming down his face; his whole body was wet. Dancing in the Park was one thing; running hotfoot down these closed-in streets was another. He hoped that none of his elevator boys or the night doorman had been standing outside seeing him chasing a girl up the street in the middle of the night, and Patty just sailed this afternoon.

But where had she gone? He turned into the foyer of his apartment house, in order not to pass it. He'd beetle up to the corner in a second to see if she was racing up Park Avenue. But he heard the voice of Bauers the new superintendent raised in an angry shout, and Bauers himself, in shirt sleeves, warm and wroth, was denouncing someone who had just vanished around the corner at the rear in the direction of service and the superintendent's basement apartment.

"A fine time for you to be coming home, young lady! Your ma's been half crazy. Said you was going out for a walk and it's after one. Where you been?"

A voice from the rear. "Oh, shut up, Pa. I been to the Park."

"Park! I'll learn you to bum around in the P——"

He saw Career. He coughed apologetically. "Excuse me, Mr. Career. My shirt sleeves and all. I was just worrying about my daughter, where she was. Of course it's hot down in the basement where we live, but young folks nowdays, honest to God, Mr. Career, I don't know what they're coming to."

"That's right," agreed Alan Career feebly. Bauers himself took him up in the elevator, still apologizing. Bauers said it was too hot to sleep and that's a fact. Career said, vaguely, was it, and Mr. Bauers decided privately that he had been drinking. You could smell it on his breath, and his face was like a beet.

He let himself into the apartment, he flicked on the light, he stood there swaying a little as if he were drunk, which he was not. The place was stifling. He felt as if he were choking. Ice water. That was it. He went to the kitchen. Dahlia's room off the kitchen was dark and her door open. The back hall door was not chained from the inside. She hadn't come in yet. He poured a glass of water from the iced bottle in the refrigerator, dumped ice into it, swallowed it thirstily and then another though the chill burned his throat and made it ache. As he was closing the refrigerator door he saw a little saucedish of red raspberries looking rosily up at him, sugared and tempting. Holding out on him, was she? Thought he'd had the whole box for dinner. Saving this for his breakfast, probably. He got a spoon and ate the saucerful, leaving the icebox comfortably open until its warning burr protested against such treatment. He put the plate and spoon in the sink.

A cold bath before he turned in. Nope, couldn't stand it, too tired. He peeled his clothes, he lay a moment staring at the empty bed next his all primly dressed in its dotted-swiss summer flounces. He turned out the light and rolled over.

The superintendent's daughter. If Patty ever knew she'd have a stroke. . . . Poor little kid.

FOOD

THE SWIEBACKS had everything lovely. Or almost everything. Mrs. Swieback would have been—was, in fact—the first to tell you so.

"We got everything lovely. The apartment you couldn't ask for anything grander, we can see the Park from our bathroom, around the corner it practically is from us. Either I or the girl takes little Manning every day he should play by the pond in the grass, it's perfect. My Mannie is a gorgeous husband and father, if I say so. I don't want to brag. Even I don't have to open my mouth to ask for something already I got it. I was born lucky, like Mannie says I am shot with luck, it's a slang expression. All my life I wanted to live on the East Side —I mean below Hundert and Tenth, naturally—and so

I'm living, the hall downstairs, the foyer, it's like a palace especially in the winter with Turkish rugs and drapes and everything done in Italian, the furniture. I got tickets the fourth Monday regular as clockwork we go to the Guild opening, not the opening night it isn't of course, but for us subscribers it is like an opening till the tickets are for sale with outsiders like you. I got my mink, Manning goes like a little prince, everything at Best's. But what is the good—I got no husband. Well, I don't mean I ain't got my Mannie, God forbid. But on Saturday night only, like a fella, not a husband. It's the business. I ought to be ashamed to talk like that about a grand business brings us in such a wonderful living. Ony it's like I am married and got no husband, God forbid. Mannie, he does all the buying fruit and vegetables for the whole three stores. It is some job. One o'clock in the middle of the night he is got to be up to go to Washington Market, it's downtown by the river. So daytime he sleeps, it's like you was married to a mill hand, or something. I shouldn't ought to say that, a king like my Mannie. Five six o'clock in the morning he comes home, he has got to sleep again. Day in, day out, ony Saturday nights he can sleep like a person, account Sunday is closed the stores, naturally. Ony he can't sleep because he is by now so used to sleeping crazy like that he wakes up anyway the same as usual. Sunday mornings he just lays there like a mouse so he doesn't wake me but I hear him anyway. Him and little Manning—he is got his own room, Manning—they can't wink a eyelash I don't hear it right away. I am like that. Day in, day out, so it goes like that. The worst is he don't hardly see little Manning his own son from one week's end to the other. He leaves, the boy is asleep, naturally. He comes home the boy is in bed. It's sh-sh-sh! you wake your papa, all the time. Manning might as well got no papa, God forbid, ony Sundays. Oh, well, I couldn't complain when I see what others got and how grand I got it, Mannie a wonderful provider and the sun rises and sets in me and Manning, and this gorgeous apartment on Lexington and a maid—the girl she can't cook anything extra but that I don't mind, I like to cook, she is with little Manning wonderful, she is crazy about the child, you would think she is the mother, not me. Yes, we got everything lovely, if ony Mannie didn't have to get up such a hour, rain or shine, summer and winter.

Every morning till five and six down there in that place, it's like crazy. A hour for a grand man like my Mannie he should be up!"

This July night Mannie Swieback had slept badly for the day and the night had been insufferably hot. He had awakened at ten, at eleven, at twelve, he had lain there, tortured with heat and sleeplessness. And even when he slept, fitfully, he muttered in his sleep. Delphine Swieback (Della to her folks) listened and made out his mumblings to be about raspberries. My poor darling always the business on his mind. Raspberries. Suddenly he shouted, "Raspberries!" in quite a loud voice so that he woke himself up and sat upright in his bed sweating freely and staring wildly about in the midnight blackness.

"Sh-sh, Mannie, you wake the child!"

She got up and padded heavily into the adjoining room, but the round brown sausage that was Manning II (out of Emanuel) lay peacefully asleep in his bed, his breathing steady, his chest and belly barrel-like with good living from the Aye Wun Stores, Emanuel Swieback, Prop.

His wife and child came first, of course. But the

business was part of him, part of them all, it was his first thought when he wakened, his last when he fell asleep. All through the day he was immersed in it, happy as a fish in water. Sometimes he wondered if the name—Aye Wun Stores—was quite the thing. It had been all right up in the Bronx where he had started. But now with a store on Lexington near Seventy-first and another at Eighty-sixth and still another at Fifty-sixth and Third he had his doubts. Something like The De Luxe Markets would have been the thing. But that Sophy Lieber called her market by that name. The Widow Lieber, his ruthless enemy and competitor on Lexington. In gold letters on the Aye Wun plate-glass store windows you read, Long Island And Westchester Deliveries Tuesday Thursday Saturday. He had even contemplated adding Newport to these gold letters, but he had decided against it, though reluctantly. These deliveries were mostly mythical for his customers could avail themselves of local markets near their summer homes. But it was true that when they wanted something special, something rare, something precious in the food line, then the Aye Wun Stores, Emanuel Swieback, Prop., could supply it. Mannie made a specialty of fruits, vegetables, and poultry out of season. No dainty too exquisite, no source too remote, for his providing. The Widow Lieber had been quick to follow his lead in this and the rivalry between them was of vendetta proportions. The neighborhood was what Mannie called classy. A customer caught with a rare dainty was often a customer gained for life. If It's Edible The Aye Wun Has It, was the store motto. It was becoming difficult to get things out of season because now practically everything seemed to be in season all the year round. New York palates were overpampered.

"It used to be," Mannie complained, "you got watermelon in August and grapes in September and strawberries in June and spring chickens in the spring and turkeys at Thanksgiving and so on. But now! Turkeys you get in May, and strawberries in January, and peaches in March and all of them the year around. Folks is spoiled, thank God. Now it is so if you got something in season in season, you understand, why it's considered out of season. A crazy world."

Now, at Mannie's nocturnal shouts Mrs. Swieback was disturbed but not too distressed. She knew it was business on his mind. And the heat. She came back to bed now. "You woke yourself up, Mannie, with your business worries. Isn't that a foolishness! What you want to worry? We got everything lovely. Leave be. Raspberries! Who cares raspberries!"

"I tell you what," he said to the plump black-haired armful in the vaguely French bed beside his own, "I tell you what, it's too hot you and Mannie staying here in New York. You go up to the mountains anyway a month."

"And leave you here alone in the flat, with that girl's cooking, and if you should get sick! If it ain't too hot you should stand it it ain't too hot for me. And Manning is brown and healthy like a Indian—knock on wood."

He rose now, for it was nearly one o'clock, and began to dress hurriedly like a soldier going into battle, with necessity for speed but reluctance to face the turmoil. "I'm going down early, I can't sleep anyway, the heat. And I want I should get the first chance at the raspberries."

"Raspberries, raspberries!" echoed Mrs. Swieback in sleepy irritation. "What is it with raspberries all the time! Never in all my life have I heard so much from raspberr——" But she was caught up in sleep like a living Rubens painting, all black hair and scarlet cheeks and white flesh on the tumbled sheets.

He rarely stopped even for a cup of coffee. He could get that later, in the market. He went to the garage around the corner and got the little battered car. He wouldn't dream of using the good car that he and Delphine had for evenings and occasional Sunday driving. They scarcely used it even then, for that matter. It was more a symbol than a toy or a convenience. Mannie was dressed a trifle shabbily, too, for the night's fray. But though the suit was shabby it was well made, and so was his shirt, but they were old and unfit for his wearing in any place other than Washington Market with its slippery streets, its piled-up produce, its rush and almost savage strife.

He was not a dashing driver; Mannie had no head for mechanics. He eased his pudgy figure behind the wheel now, then sat tense and watchful as he trundled down the streets. Over to Park, down to Fourteenth, across to Twelfth, past the docks of the steamship lines and the freight sheds. The waters of the North

River were almost hidden by the great piers and warehouses; only now and then you had a glimpse of it, smooth and oily under the hot July night sky.

As always, he had some difficulty in finding a parking place, though he left his car on the fringe of the Washington Market maelstrom. The Aye Wun trucks would pick up his purchased merchandise, both fruit and vegetables. But they were somewhere within the battle line itself by now. His notebook and order book in his pocket, a cigarette between his lips, he went forward into battle, a gargoyle little figure, shrewd, sentimental. The short bandy legs bespoke an undernourished childhood down on New York's swarming East Side; the round belly and the plump cheeks testified to his marital content and his present affluent state. A bad foundation, a top-heavy upper part; but the sound heart and kidneys would see him through.

Half-past one. Washington Market was a brilliant bazaar—a mass of color and sound and fury. Thousands of men labored here all night so that New York's millions should be fed next day. From midnight until six in the morning it was the most vital spot in all New York; it was more male than Wall Street itself at mid-day. Every street—north and south, east and west—in the Washington Market area was chock-a-block. A thousand vast trucks loomed up like freight cars, their rubber-shod double wheels proportioned like a juggernaut's. Drays, vans, carts, wagons, horses were wedged like pieces in a jigsaw puzzle. Huge draft-horses, pudding footed, clopped the pavement in a day when a horse was thought to be an anachronism. On the driver's seat of the great trucks backed up at the curb men lay asleep in the midst of incredible turmoil as the load was being taken off. They had driven these hundreds of tons a distance of fifty, a hundred, one hundred and fifty miles that day; they would drive back tonight; tomorrow they would repeat the trip with a fresh load. They must snatch repose where they could. Food for millions, perishable, costly, it must be moved before the sun was high. By seven the streets would be almost empty, by noon as deserted as the catacombs. Hard tough concentrated work; shrewd competitive realistic men.

Through this brilliant carnival of color and sound Mannie Swieback made his way. It required lively stepping and expert dodging as the siren of an ambulance occasionally testified. The pavement was slippery, the sidewalks worse, the street crossings were blocked so that he was forced to worm his way in and out of a tangle of vehicles. All about was the stamping of iron-shod hoofs on stone; the rattling of trace chains, the snort of engines, the nerve-racking report of backfire, the rumble of heavy barrows, the shouts and yells of men.

On the sidewalks outside the commission houses were piled boxes and bales, crates, bags, baskets of fruits and vegetables. They were stacked higher than a man's head, forming narrow perilous aisles for pedestrians. Down these aisles charged a constant stream of giant Negroes pushing laden hand trucks. These they kept upright by some miracle of balancing skill. The muscles stood out on their bare black arms and chests, their eyes rolled and seemed to start from their sockets with the strain of the load. "Watch it!" they yelled not a second too soon as a buyer or commission man leaped nimbly to flatten himself against a bank of boxed lettuce or oranges or apples.

Mannie was looking for his own trucks and drivers. They had an approximate stand, but one never knew from night to night what luck the crowded street might bring. Force and ingenuity and ruthlessness decided the location of your truck. As he squirmed and dodged to avoid this driver, that hurtling box, Mannie kept a sharp and experienced eye on the night's produce. This was the height of the summer season. Even August would bring no greater variety of growing things. Melons from North Carolina. Cherries from Oregon. Peaches from Colorado. Pears, apples, oranges, strawberries. The currants were the size of cherries, the cherries as big as plums. Peas and beans from Jersey. Eggplant from Virginia, iridescent purple like an oriental empress, too majestic to be mere food. Cauliflower like a bride's bouquet. Carrots, onions, potatoes, lettuce, celery; leeks, corn, spinach, asparagus, alligator pears. Tops of sample boxes were laid craftily open so that the rosy cheeks and plump firm flesh caught the eye of the passing buyer and tempted him, as slaves were displayed on the block in the far East. Vitamins for swarming New York in July; the lettuce in a drugstore sandwich; the tomatoes in a noonday salad; the greens for soup; the mint in Alan Career's julep, the peppers for his corn sauté. The raspberries——

No raspberries, dusty red and downy like the lips of a Spanish beauty. Huckleberries, yes; blackberries, unseasonable strawberries. "What's the matter no raspberries?" Mannie demanded of this commissioner and that. The commission men in white aprons and straw hats stood outside their doorways, plump and rosy as their own fruits. They smoked large cigars nervously.

"Well, I tell you, Mannie, they ain't none. How about some nice blackberries, I got some extra select huckle——"

But he was off down the street, poking, smelling, pinching. Raspberries. He had to have raspberries for the week-end trade. Raspberries to pour, crushed, over their Sunday ice cream at dinner; or for the heaped-up bowl at breakfast. His Park Avenue trade wanted raspberries because they were scarce and expensive. Only yesterday that colored girl from the Careers, she had come in, she is got to have raspberries. Peaches, currants, huckleberries, blackberries—no. The boss says raspberries he wants. And who has got raspberries? Nobody on the whole street, nobody on the East Side only that Lieber, that black widow Lieber. She must, then, have got them from Sam Klug, that cutthroat, a widower, he was always after Lieber, that cow; everybody knew he wanted to marry her only for her good business.

Morosely he dug a plump finger into a watermelon's broad sides. "Heh, watch it!" A hand truck overturned with a crash as the fore wheel tipped crazily negotiating the high curb and encountered a backing van.

Out of nowhere appeared Garbage Hannah with her string bag. She was a nightly prowler. Her rheumy eye scanned the curbs and the sidewalks for stray greens and bits of fruit—a carrot loosened from the pile, an orange half crushed under a horse's hoof, an apple that had rolled into the gutter. Into the string bag they went. No one knew whether she ate this refuse or sold it. She roamed and searched, and cursed the truckmen when they hooted at her. Bet she's got a million dollars, the Market was fond of saying. I bet when old Garbage Hannah dies they find about seventy bank books and her trunk choked with twenty-dollar bills. I bet she's stinkin' with dough. They always are.

As Mannie searched he did not waste time. He bought, too, his transactions brief and his conversation terse; out came his notebook. The truck would pick up the stuff later. Here, there, everywhere he trotted, scenting a delicacy, ferreting out a rare lot of fruit or a consignment of vegetables made scarce by the withering heat.

He came to Sam Klug's place, its front piled high with every conceivable fruit, the lights beating down from the roof of the protecting shed. Sam himself, irate in the doorway.

"Hi, get that truck outta there!" An empty truck was wedged just in front of the curb, locked there, seemingly, in a hopeless jam of cars and wagons and vans.

The driver surveyed the teeming street, he cast a look of scorn on Klug. "Yeh, where 'll I put it!" he yelled. No one spoke, merely, in Washington Market; they yelled. It was part of the technique of the whole opera.

The answer to this was obvious. Mr. Klug was not one to deny himself a conversational opening such as this. He told him.

"A minute," interrupted Mannie. "That's my truck. What's the matter all of a sudden you're so high and mighty he's got to move——" Then he remembered his errand. Diplomacy, not rancor, must be the keynote. "Look, Sam, you got right he's blocking the street. I'll see he gets away from there. Only first let's do a little business, h'm? You ain't too busy to sell something, maybe?" The crook. The murderer. Widows he's got to have, yet. A honest father of a family isn't good enough for a customer.

He bought this and that to cover his real purpose.

"Seen Sophy Lieber?" he inquired with crafty casualness. "I got a message for her."

"Not this evening I ain't. I'm expecting her any minute, though."

So. If there were raspberries hidden away for her by her suitor she had not yet secured them.

"Uh—how much for them strawberries? Watery."

"Ten to you."

"Keep 'em."

He closed his notebook, he made as though to leave. "Now I'll get that fella out of there for you—oh, by the way, I need a few raspberries. How's your raspberries?"

"No raspberries."

"I got to have a few raspberries just to dress the

window, y'understand. I can't make a cent on 'em and I don't expect to. So come on. I'll pay for them."

"What do you mean—got to! It's been raining, all of a sudden it is hot enough to burn everything on the vines—they ain't no raspberries. If they ain't raspberries so people do without seeing them in the window of the Aye Wun Market."

"Yes, but that's just the trouble, Sam. People don't want to do without. They go till they get them somewhere and it's maybe a customer lost. I pay any price. You know me when I want something. I'm no piker. So come on now, Sam, hustle out that crate raspberries you're holding out on me. You can't fool Mannie Swieback."

"All right, I got a crate. Just one. But I already promised 'em."

"Who to?"

"What's the difference who to—they ain't for sale." Coyly. The rhinoceros.

"Look, Sam, I ask you as a favor. To you maybe it's nothing. To me, either I got the choicest things in and out of season in my market on the swell East Side, or I ain't."

"Well, then, you ain't."

Mannie now threw pretense to the winds. "Look. If Soph—if the Dee Looks don't want 'em will you let me have 'em? That's fair enough, ain't it? If she—if they don't come for them by, say, four o'clock—it's after three now—will you sell 'em to me?"

"If the berries is still here at four you can have 'em."

"No, that ain't good enough. I says, if the Dee Looks hasn't picked them up by four will you save them for me, word of honor?"

Sam Klug now assumed an injured air and appealed to the sense of justice of an imaginary audience. "Listen to him! He don't trust a man I've been dealing with him for how many years! Did you ever——"

"You will or you won't . . . Here—Mike!" He called to the boy on the truck backed against the curb. "If by four o'clock the Dee Looks, God forbid, ain't picked up a crate raspberries here with Sam Klug, you get 'em and hang on to 'em, you hear?"

"All right, all right," said Klug, still injured innocence. "But she—the Dee Looks wants them."

"He'll watch," Mannie threatened grimly. And was off.

He had bought prodigiously for the week-end trade but now this single crate of berries loomed more important than all the rest. The artist in Mannie Swieback was aroused. Perfection or nothing. The most infuriating thought was that his rival was a woman—the one woman buyer in Washington Market. It was no place for a woman. Why didn't she let a manager or a man buyer come down here in this crazy market and do her buying? No, she had to come. She took a shameful advantage of her sex. Not that the Widow Lieber was lovely or alluring. She was a monster, swarthy, big-bosomed, broad-hipped, sharp-tongued. Her husband had died, leaving her with the business and two children. A formidable woman, ruthless as an Amazon, tireless, working all day, all night. The son was to go to college. The daughter was training to be a dancer. Talented, Sophy said. Unusual, her children. All right, if she wanted to work like a man let her take a man's chances in the Market.

He was hungry now, but he would not stop to eat. He passed the lunchrooms that dotted the streets, their neon lights beckoning him, their smells enticing to a breakfastless man. A cup of coffee was what he craved, but he put the thought aside. Later. Inside the lunchrooms the truck drivers were fortifying themselves against the long drive home. They wolfed gargantuan breakfasts on this hot July morning; pigs' knuckles and sauerkraut, liver and bacon, ham and eggs, beef stew swimming in gravy, mops of bread; coffee and coffee rings. The scent of the coffee was too much for Mannie. He darted into the Ritz lunch and swallowed a burning cup of heavily creamed coffee and a coffee ring. Immediately he felt livelier, more confident. He sallied forth again to the fray.

"Cigarscigaretteschewinggumcandy!" The battered visage of Cigarette Sarah with her basket appeared around a small mountain of crates. He bought a packet of cigarettes just for luck, told her to keep the change out of a quarter, and shuddered away from her witch-like grin. On the sidewalk in front of a closed warehouse door a group of colored boys were shooting craps with murmured adjurations and rolling eyes. Mannie paused a moment to look over a shoulder and the boy won. A good sign. "Stay here wid me, boss!" said the boy. But he hurried on. He peered into the open door of every commission house, he stared at every group on the sidewalk. He even told himself that he was being foolish—crazy with the heat, Mannie, he thought. But he went on.

There she was at last, a massive unlovely mountain of flesh in her gingham dress tightly strained across her tumultuous bosom; wrinkled brown stockings, a battered straw hat of no determinate age or sex. She was standing at the shelf-desk in Louie Pinello's place writing in her order book and stowing a memorandum away in the capacious pocket of her skirt. She did not bother with so feminine an adjunct as a handbag, this formidable female. Mannie entered breezily.

"Hiyah, Louie! Hi, Sophy! How's the little woman?"

She threw him a brief and malevolent look and went on copying. Chunk of suet, Mannie thought. A woman! "I ain't seen you lately, Mrs. Lieber. I thought maybe you wasn't coming down these days, such heat, a woman."

"Heat or no heat, a woman is got to live the same as a man."

Mannie laughed at this and wagged his head in admiring agreement. "You got me there, Sophy. Well, how's about a cup of coffee with me? I was just going to have one."

"I got no time for coffee," the fair widow rasped sourly.

"Okay. No offense, my girl," benevolently. He now raised his voice well above the clamor of the streets, addressing Louie in a more masculine tone as it were. "How about blackberries, Louie?" Then, before Louie could answer Mannie held up a plump palm and continued, "—and when I say blackberries, Louie, I ask blackberries so don't tell me you got red raspberries as big as tomatoes because I ain't in the market to buy poison raspberries, so don't think you can unload raspberries on Mannie Swieback."

Out of the tail of his eye he saw Sophy's busy pencil slow its caperings.

"Raspberries!" snorted Louie Pinello. "You know damn well I nor nobody else ain't got raspberries, and if they did——"

"You don't have to tell me. I know. If they did they'd have poison and not raspberries. I guess Louie Pinello is too smart a boy to get himself put in jail for a child poisoner like the fella in this morning's paper."

Sophy's pencil was still. Her back was toward him but it was vibrant with attention.

Louie Pinello stared. "What do you mean—child poisoning?"

Mannie only laughed. "No, you don't know. Certainly not!"

Sophy Lieber now abandoned pretense. She turned slowly, ponderously, like a freighter changing its course. Her face was a mask of suspicion. Mannie, that superb actor, now appeared to abandon the subject. He cut through Louie Pinello's amazed protests. "These here huckleberries you got, Louie. My opinion, they ain't so hot, but——"

"What do you mean—poison?" Sophy demanded with elephantine directness.

"Huh?" said Mannie, absent-mindedly, as though deep in other thoughts. He nibbled a huckleberry between his strong yellow teeth.

"You heard me. What do you mean, poison in the morning papers, raspberries!"

"Don't you read the paper, Sophy? You got your mind always too much on money and business, you get into trouble yet, mark my words. You get a million dollars, what good does it do you if you are in jail and your children disgraced forever!"

She shouted now like any truck driver. "What are you talking, you big mouth! If you don't—what are you talking, poison and jail!"

"Sh-sh! Sophy! What is with you? I was just saying, no offense. They're all poison. Maybe they hushed it up in the later editions. I get the early morning paper, first thing when I drive down. They're all poison it said. That's why you can't buy a crate raspberries—or a box, that matter—for love or money. Scairt to sell them, scairt to buy them. Naturally."

"It's a lie. Raspberries is scarce account the wet weather and now the heat."

"All right, Soph. It's all right by me. Ony the paper says raspberry blight, it is very seldom it happens, the growers they used some kind of spray, it had poison in it not only it kills the blight it kills who eats the raspberries, even washed. So the food officers say it's forbidden raspberries, and they lay in the warehouses, rotting. Of course, a crate might not have the blight at all, then again it might be enough to kill a whole family. Family! Say! A neighborhood! Convulsions they get first, it's terrible. I don't take no chances. Believe me, huckleberries is good enough for Mannie

Swieback's customers this week end." He turned. "Hi, Louie! Where's that loafer? I ain't got all night and day I should spend over a handful huckleberries."

Louie Pinello laughed scornfully. "I never heard such a lot of hooey in my life. You're nuts, Mannie."

Mannie surveyed him more in sorrow than in anger. "Am I a stool pigeon or something, Louie, you got to be afraid to talk in front of me? You ain't got any raspberries. I ain't got any raspberries. The Widow Lieber here ain't——" A sudden terrible suspicion then seemed to dart like an adder through his mind. "Sophy, my poor woman, you ain't stuck with a lot of poison raspberries, are you? Bought and paid for? Somebody didn't do that to a woman is trying to make a living for herself and her childr——"

"No!" snarled Sophy Lieber. "I am too smart for that. I am as smart as you are any day, Mr. Mannie Swieback. I knew all the time they was poison. Say, what do you think? I can't read!"

Mannie smiled affably at this and wagged his head again in silent admiration. He breathed a deep sigh. He looked about him with an air of finality. "Well, I guess I go home. I'm just about finished up for the day. . . .

You look tired, Mrs. Lieber. It's terrible work for a woman, the Market. I'm surprised you don't marry again—a fine woman like you. I hear there is plenty grand boys would be glad to marry you and run the business for you and be a father to your wonderful children. I hear that Sam Klug—there is a wonderful fella for you, I hear he is crazy about——"

"Klug!" roared the Widow Lieber, a tinge of purple enriching the already ruddy color in her cheeks. "That bum! That cutthroat! Him I don't go near, even to buy!"

She charged out of the shop. Mannie Swieback, humming a little tune, followed her leisurely to the doorway and stood idly a moment watching the ponderous figure waddling up the street away from the direction of Sam Klug's commission house.

GARBAGE

He was being pursued by devils with English plaid socks over their hoofs. Beating cymbals to the tune of

Whoa Babe they chased him through the Park to Trinity churchyard calling attention to the fact that he was stark naked in the midst of Wall Street's noonday throng. The girl stenographers perched on the ancient gravestones eating their lunches with elegantly crooked little fingers jumped up at sight of him and joined in the chase, only suddenly it was he who was chasing them.

Alan Career awoke in a hot and cold sweat—hot because of the temperature of the sweltering July morning; cold because of terror. He found himself half out of bed, one foot on the floor, the other flexed for running as he used to gauge his stride when he was the crack man in the hurdles and the four-forty dash at the Interscholastic Field Meet in Chillicothe, Ohio.

He sat there on the edge of his bed breathing fast, as though he actually had been running. His hand went to his forehead in fright and bewilderment and the palm came away wet. The bedroom was hot, bright, breathless. He looked at his watch. Seven o'clock. The clashing noise that, in his nightmare, had been devils' cymbals now resolved itself into an actual sound. It was a sound all too familiar to New York apartment dwellers. Fiends of another sort were at work in their gifted way. The garbage men were collecting the morning cans.

In a neighborhood such as the Careers' they always came around two hours later than this. A region inhabited by the wealthy and late-sleeping, the Department of Sanitation knew that the clatter of early garbage and ashcans would result in too many telephone calls from highly indignant voices threatening to report the outrage to their friend the Mayor and their friend the Chief of Police.

"Leave 'em lay," the order had gone forth from the new Department of Sanitation Head. It was the lesser neighborhoods, the more obscure streets, the walk-up apartments that submitted to the six and seven o'clock clatter and bang.

But this, they must have figured, was summer, and the occupants of the proud piles absent in some cool haven redolent of balsam and far removed from such urban vulgarities as ash and garbage cans. The shaded and shuttered windows on Fifth and Park and the stately side streets testified to the soundness of this reasoning. And now toss and catch, with a high percentage of misses, seemed to be going on below Alan Career's bedroom window, three stories up. (The higher the dearer in New York's rental arithmetic.)

As if this were not enough, one of the tossers or catchers was singing at the top of a not very true tenor voice the more difficult passages from Pagliaccio's lament.

Alan Career staggered to the window unmindful of the fact that he had slept minus a pajama top. He stuck his head out into the glaring heat of the day. Five hours of sleep! Five hours after a day like yesterday.

"Heh, you! Yes, you! What the hell do you mean yapping and banging and waking people up in the middle of the night!"

There were three men on the wagon: one driving, two wrestling cans. It was one of those modern garbage trucks, smart, enamelled, buff colored, discreetly hooded and as different from the old odorous one-horse affair as an airplane is unlike a prairie schooner. The song broke off abruptly. The three looked up at the tousled head and the bare brown torso protruding from the stately edifice of brick and stone. They were silent. They fell into frozen attitudes of attention like privates when an officer catches them off guard. Indeed, they wore khaki-colored uniforms and their caps had a military aspect. One—the one who had been singing—had a jaunty sprig of mountain laurel stuck in his cap band. It was this one who said, "Sorry, mister." The face upturned to Alan Career's window was boyish, olive-skinned, and cameo-cut, with a profile designed for the movies. Career, wide awake now, suddenly wished he hadn't bawled out of the window at these men working.

The second man of the pair who had been hurling ashcans now grinned and pointed to the singer. "Tony's feeling good. He's going to be married tomorrow."

Alan Career thought that Pagliacci was not quite the medium through which to express a state of amorous joy. He felt a fresh pang of remorse. "Well, what do you know about that!" he said, inadequately.

The man at the wheel now entered the conversation which was taking on the aspect of an urban version of a small-town back fence gossip interlude. "Yeh, and he's through tomorrow."

"Fired?" yelled Alan Career, shocked.

"Fired nothin'! Promoted. Assistant foreman, that's what. Twenny-one hunderd a year. That's how he's getting married." There was vicarious pride in the voice of Tony's confrere.

Tony now took up the explanation. No one seemed to find anything odd in this casual morning scene. "We thought the building was empty, see. We figgered everybody was to the country, we'd make the rounds early and get off." As one man to another.

"Well, sure," Alan agreed, surveying the dead-eyed walls up and down the street. "I'm all alone on the island. Me and you and a few other million like us." Then a thought struck him. "You fellows come up and have a drink?"

"It ain't allowed. . . . It's against regulations."

A fresh thought now came to him; a better one. "Too early, anyway. Listen, wait a minute, will you? Don't go away. I got something for you, Tony. Wedding present."

The head was withdrawn. As he padded back to the little bar off the front hall he remembered how he used to deliver the morning papers back in Chillicothe. They came in on the early train from the city. Only the well to do took the out-of-town paper. He used to make the rounds on his bike, twisting the paper into a firm knob and hurling it at the front door with a vicious thud. "I guess that 'll wake you up," he had thought, though he hadn't known it.

Somewhere in the liquor cabinet there was a quart of champagne left over from their fifth wedding anniversary celebration. He couldn't remember how this strange phenomenon had come about. But as he rummaged and finally found it he was somewhat dashed to see that the quart was a magnum. Probably everybody had had enough, and a magnum, opened, would have been sheer waste. Patty had figured that one out. The closet contained little beside this; a bottle or two of half-emptied Scotch, some gin, some of that sweet red stuff that women put into cocktails. With a passing pang of regret he slapped barefooted back to the window and held up the bottle. "Minute!" he shouted. About the neck of the bottle he firmly knotted a corner of his bed sheet making a cradle of it. He then knotted a second sheet to a corner of the first. Inspired by his own brilliance his roving eye now hit upon the fourteen-foot telephone cord with which Patty liked to roam about the bedroom when conversing with friends on the wire; now telephoning from her bed, now from the dressing table, now from the chaise longue. With some difficulty he tied the cord, its mouthpiece dangling, to the sheet end and gently, cautiously, lowered his fragile glass burden foot by foot out of the window to the region of the sidewalk below. There it hung, a surprising object, within easy reach of Tony's nimble brown fingers.

Alan Career bawled a final message before he hauled up his ingenious rope. "It's for your wedding. Health to the bride and groom, see! Put it on ice. It's got to be cold. Ice!" He withdrew his head. Despairing of further sleep he turned on the cold-water bath tap.

Tony Marucci looked at the vast rounded sides of the big green bottle in his hands. He spelled out the word letter by letter. B-o-l-l-i-n-g-e-r. 1921. Champagne.

"It's wine," he announced to his curious mates. "Champagne wine. What do you figger he wanted to go to work and do that for?"

"Hangover."

"No, he talked all right, only nothing on."

"I bet it ain't any good."

"No, he was an all-right guy. He just felt like giving away, and he thought of this."

"Let's see. Whyn't you open it?"

"Nope. Health of the bride and groom, the guy says. And that's how it's going to be."

The equipage, garbage laden, rolled ponderously down the street, Tony's sprig of mountain laurel, plucked from who knows what ashcan, nodding gaily in the sun.

In the Department of Sanitation they called them G Men, facetiously. But the G Men were proud of their occupation. A good city job, and no limit, practically, to your chances of promotion. Hadn't Ben Gourley himself, now Head of the Sanitation Department of the City of New York, started collecting garbage back in the days when there was one man to a wagon, and that wagon a crude two-wheeled lumbering affair drawn by one decrepit nag? At department banquets and picnics Ben liked to reminisce about those days when he was driver, collector, and dumper, working from six in the morning until six or even eight at night, and all for fourteen dollars a week, and glad to get it. The hundreds of hard-muscled G Men listened respectfully. You said it, they thought. They knew that after three years as collector you were in line for Assistant Foreman at $2,100 a year if your record was tops. After that, with the breaks, you could be Foreman at $2,385. Listen. You could be Superintendent at $3,085. You could be Head—— But Tony Marucci's brain always reeled at that. Not Iolanda's, though. Iolanda would be Mrs. Tony Marucci tomorrow, and her brain never reeled.

It had been Iolanda's unswerving determination and boundless ambition that had prodded Tony into his assistant foremanship. They had been "going together" since she was seventeen. She was twenty now, and Tony had been no languid suitor. But Iolanda was as unsentimental as any daughter of the new Italy. Though she never had seen her parents' native land its dictator would have approved of her.

"I'm not going to marry any guy can't give me a nice place to live and nice things. You'll be slinging garbage cans all your life if you don't figure ahead and get things started right now. I'm not going to look like Ma when I'm her age—old as a squaw and never has any fun. You get yourself a job as foreman and then we'll get married, and not before. Lots of girls would marry you right now. Well, let 'em. It ain't that I'm not crazy about you. But young people today can't be like that. Look at Pa, working for the WPA. Look at Angelica married four years and she hasn't had a new dress since, and babies all over the dump. Well, I know I sound hard-boiled but when she married Marino she married a sap. And now look. Not me. So get busy. Three years you'll be twenty-five—and Assistant Foreman."

Tony the romantic got busy. His record was flawless, he had used every ounce of influence in his precinct, he had pitched his ball team to victory, he had sung in the glee club, he was the garbage and ash man par excellence. But sometimes, during those three years, he had wished that Iolanda had had not quite so much character.

With his last load he trundled with the truck and crew into the new garbage incinerator on the far west side near the waterfront. The vast building was as bright and clean and airy as a watch factory. True, there was about it a certain acrid odor that might elevate a more sensitive and unaccustomed nose. Tony and the boys did not even notice it. They dumped the load into the receiving pit, an immense cavern that ran the length of the block-long building on the ground floor. Tony had carefully removed his great green bottle from the driver's cab up in front. Now, while the truck was being emptied, and before the truck and crew made their way uptown to report for final roll call, he went rather shyly about making his farewells. Assistant Foreman after tonight. Well, so long, Mike! Hi, Gus! Just thought I'd say good-by. He raised a palm in farewell to the furnace tenders raking the final fires of the day in the six great flaming pits. The traveling cranes overhead jerked open the yawning buckets whose jaws scooped up mouthful after mouthful of the tonnage below, dropped the stuff into the bins, the bins opened and released the mass into the furnace pits. Tony even went up the stairs that led to the bin floor. The men up there whose job it was to prod the laden bins as they emptied into the furnaces below were chained by the belt to posts. There was a job for you! The chains kept them from losing their balance and slipping over the bin edge should their poles catch and jerk them. A dumb bunch, Tony thought, for they often unbuckled their chains on the sly, though it was forbidden by the rules. Then, sometimes, they mysteriously disappeared and there was only a belt buckle or some such telltale bit of metal in the furnace siftings next day to tell the tragic, sordid tale.

"So long, boys!"

"Big boss now, eh Tony?" But their tone was not grudging.

Hugging his bottle, wrapped now in a piece of coarse brown paper, he reported at the uptown station for lineup and roll call. His last roll call as collector.

There they stood in khaki pants and brown shirts, the one hundred and fifty men of the district. The names, as they fell from the lips of the inspector, made a picture of America. The men stood straight and fit, at attention.

Polacheck? Here! Monahan? Here! Cohn? Here! Scott—Podzulski—Tonetti—Dietenhofer—Brennan—Wells—Tregouboff—Popoudopoulas? Here! here! here!

Tony made a rush for the shower and washroom. Iolanda was expecting him at five. Usually he stopped at the Elite Diner across the street for a sandwich and a cup of coffee, but not today. When he emerged an almost incredible metamorphosis had taken place. Here was a modish young blood in gray trousers, blue shirt, trim tie, perforated buckskin shoes. He had not stopped to shave. The blue-black stubble only served to enhance his Latin look of romance and virility. It was a stubborn beard and a tender skin. He'd shave twice over tomorrow morning before the wedding.

He found an extremely busy and somewhat waspish Iolanda in the crowded walk-up flat which was her home. The shop people from whom she was renting the white satin wedding dress and the voluminous cloud of trailing white net veil had said they couldn't send the outfit until midnight because it was being used for a six o'clock wedding this evening.

"Tell them to keep it," Tony advised her lightheartedly. "Let's get married just like we are, in regular clothes."

Iolanda withered him with a look. "Yeh, that would be dandy, that would be a swell wedding to wait three years for." Iolanda was having six bridesmaids in pink and her married sister Angelica, only slightly pregnant, as matron of honor. Her father, not being irked by his

WPA duties on Saturday, would give the bride away. Iolanda's head presented a strange aspect, like that of a Medusa of the machine age. It was tiered in wooden waves and all about her ears and neck hung little metal rolls that held her hair in a viselike grip. She was wearing a shapeless overall apron and a pair of run-down shoes, palpably the dregs of her wardrobe, for her clothes already hung in the closet of their own little flat in which they would sleep as bride and bridegroom tomorrow night.

Now Iolanda's distracted gaze fell upon the bulging package under Tony's arm. "What's that you got?"

Tony grinned. "Champagne for the wedding."

"What do you mean—champagne for the wedding?"

He unwrapped the bottle. He held it up so that the label on its bulging sides was plain for her to read. A look of horror came into her face. "Tony Marucci, you ain't gone and blown good money on stuff like that! You take that right——"

At the concentrated fury in her tone he hastily presented the truth.

"Fella give it to me. Guy was cuckoo or something, handed it to me out a window tied to a sheet."

"I don't believe it. Champagne! It costs money. Look, come on in here." She pushed him toward the front room and shut the door so that they were momentarily alone, with the family only in crude crayon staring down at them from gold frames on the wall. "Now come on, Tony. Where 'd you get it?"

Simply, he told her. She believed him. The story was too absurd to make up. Iolanda now examined the bottle with a calculating eye.

"And he says," Tony concluded triumphantly, "it was to drink the health of the bride and groom and to put it on ice. We'll be drinking champagne at our own wedding, Landa, like real Park Avenue millionaires."

Iolanda was still examining the oversized bottle, turning it over and over in her capable hands. That practical look which Tony knew so well was in her pretty face, making it look sharp and, somehow, older.

"We will not. How'd we look, drinking champagne, there isn't anywhere near enough with fifty people eating, and the rest drinking the red wine Pa made."

"Let's drink it now," Tony suggested. "Let's put it on ice and drink it tonight, you and me. I never tasted champagne. That's what we'll do. Or look, we'll take it home with us tomorrow night."

"No. Listen. Is this good champagne? Because if it is it's worth real money. I heard where a bottle of champagne if it's good costs as much as five dollars and this is bigger than any bottle of wine I ever saw. It's double, and more. We'll sell it and get the money for it."

Inured though he was to the practical side of his young bride's nature Tony recoiled at this. "You're crazy. Sell it! To who? Anyway, the guy says health to the bride and groom and put it on——"

"Who cares what he said? He must have been crazy, anyway. A bottle like that can bring ten dollars. Maybe fifteen. That's half a month's rent, and more. You go on right over to Crespi's place and ask him will he buy it off you."

"I will not. Fifteen dollars. Who ever heard of a bottle of wine bringing fifteen dollars? The heat's got you."

She was tired, she was cross, she was worried, she was a little scared, she was hot and her nerves were on edge. She blazed out at him now, a virago. "Tony

Marucci, you march out of here and down to Crespi's or some place with that bottle and sell it or I'll call the whole wedding off. I've saved and got me nice things and my own money for sheets and curtains that I worked three years for at Blum's. I ain't going to guzzle down no fifteen dollars in champagne when Pa's made red wine that's good enough for anybody. I mean it. I'm through." She was working at the dim little diamond chip ring on her engagement finger.

For three years he had been a browbeaten and faithful lover. Habit was strong; and this, he sensed, was a nerve-torn and desperate woman. If he could have looked into her subconscious mind he would have beheld a poisonous jumble made up of tardy wedding dress, three years' uncomfortable continence, a flat crowded with a voluble Latin family, a job made up of long days in Blum's bargain basement.

She thrust the bottle into his arms. He hated it now. He would have liked to smash it on the pavement. He would have liked to smash it over the head of that nut that had let it down out of the window. Sullen, morose, he walked miserably down the street toward Crespi's. Masculine wisdom told that if this bottle really was worth what his shrewd fiancée said it was then Crespi would have no use for it. Crespi's neighborhood had no call for double bottles of champagne. Tony saw himself trudging shamefacedly from liquor store to liquor store, probably farther and farther removed from his own squalid neighborhood, trying to dispose of this burden of riches like a thief with a too-rare jewel.

He stood outside Crespi's liquor store, wavering as though he had drunk the contents of the bottle in his arms. He went in. In a neighborhood largely talented enough in the making of its own wine Crespi's was a thinnish stock, and unimpressive. Rafe Crespi emerged from the murk of the back room which probably explained the existence of his shop. He eyed the great green bottle which Tony now unwrapped for his inspection. He looked at its label. His glance traveled up to Tony's flushed face.

"So what?"

"How much 'll you give me for it?"

"I ain't got no call for stuff like that around here." He stared at Tony now, suspiciously. "Is that the real stuff?"

"Well, sure. What do you think!"

"I ain't buying no Bollinger '21 champagne. You must work in a night club or something, with a bottle like that to hock. Bottle like that is worth twenty-five bucks in a night-club joint. What do you think I am? A fence!"

He walked deliberately back to the curtained rear room.

Ordinarily Tony would have hit him or any man who talked to him like that. But his anger now was transferred to the absent Iolanda. She had got him into this. But twenty-five dollars for a bottle of wine! Je's!

He wrapped it in its paper. He hated it. He wanted to drop it on the sidewalk. He passed the diner run by George the Greek, and the tantalizing smell of frying hamburgers was wafted out to his grateful nostrils. He had missed that five-o'clock coffee and sandwich and now he was suddenly ravenous. He slid onto a stool in front of the shiny white slab and placed the bottle awkwardly at his elbow where it loomed gigantic among the pygmy salts and peppers and ketchups. Things were sizzling on the flat black surface of the stove behind the counter. George the Greek greeted him, his hamburger turner in his hand. "Hi, Tony! How's the boy!" His eye fell on the vast green bottle whose paper wrapping had slipped, revealing its majestic bulging sides. "What you got there! Mineral water?"

"It's champagne. Bottle of champagne," Tony said wretchedly. "Give me a couple hamburgers, German fried, cup of coffee."

"Yeh, champagne!" jeered George the Greek. The men eating at the counter now looked up, eyeing the bottle, their mouths full.

"All right," Tony said hotly. "If it ain't champagne what is it then?" And tore away the brown paper. Bottle, label stood revealed to the full moist eye of George the Greek. George had been a bus boy at Reisenweber's over twenty years ago when bottles like this had actually circulated. He read the label with its name and date. His mouth dropped open. He stared at Tony.

"What's matter, you been robbing the Ritz or something!"

"Is it any good?" Tony asked miserably.

"Ha! Is Bollinger good! Look, twenny-five dollars

they used to get for a bottle like that at Reisenweber's, it wasn't no fifteen year old, neither. What you doing with it?"

"Nothing."

"Saving it for the wedding, eh, Tony? Some swell wedding, champagne."

"No."

George the Greek was now frankly curious. He slapped an order of ham and eggs on a plate, he cut a wedge of peach pie, slid them along the counter to their various destinations, and returned, fascinated, to this reminder of former glories. "Well, what you going to do? Huh? Wash the hair in it?"

"If it was cold," Tony said loftily, "I'd drink it. It's got to be cold, on ice."

"Sure thing. I know. Look, I'll put it on ice for you. Half an hour it's cold as hell."

"I'd look good sitting here half an hour."

"Go on next door get a shave. You look like a crook or something, them whiskers. Go on. I'll serve your hamburgers to somebody else and make you fresh. Be a sport. Where 'd you get it, anyway?"

"Fella give it to me, wedding present. My girl, she

don't—uh—she don't like champagne." A sudden thought struck him. He'd get rid of it. He waved an arm to include the counter company. "Look, everybody 'll have a drink. Stick it on ice good, George. I'll be right back."

A shave. Hot and cold towel, though the weather was smothering. He'd have another tomorrow. You only got married once. Looked like once would be enough, he reflected grimly. He tipped the barber a quarter in a gesture of defiance toward Iolanda, and felt strangely better for it.

Back at George the Greek's he found that though some of his fellow diners had eaten and gone there were others who had learned of the mysterious bottle. George was twirling it in an ice-filled mop bucket which served as cooler.

"That's-a boy! Now you look swell, like you ought to be drinking champagne. Same order?"

"Do hamburgers go good with champagne?"

"Sure. Anything goes good with champagne." George gave the bottle a final twirl in the crushed ice, but there was a little worried frown between his eyes. "Ain't no glasses, you'll have to drink it out of tumblers, it don't taste so good. It ought to have fine glasses like this." His hands described in the air fragile-stemmed glasses, bubble-bowled.

He poured a tumblerful and it brimmed over, the foam forming a pool on the counter. He dropped a small piece of ice into the glass as a precaution. "Set 'em up!" commanded Tony. "Have one yourself."

"Not for me," three or four said. Three others only drank with him and George.

Tony tossed down the tumblerful as though it were beer and he thirsty. The others followed suit, all except George the Greek. He sipped his. A look of having been cheated now came over the faces of the drinkers. "Thanks, buddy, but if that's champagne I'll take beer for mine, or a slug of whisky. It tastes like ginger pop."

"It sure does," Tony agreed, bewildered. He began to eat his hamburger and German fried, a disillusioned man.

"That ain't the way," George the Greek protested. "You got to drink it slow, like this, a sip, and taste it. Ah!" He smacked his lips and put down his glass. Then he poured another bumper for Tony. "Try that. It's colder. And not so fast."

Tony drank the glass thoughtfully. Slowly a thousand years of wine-drinking ancestors who had grown the grapes on the sun-drenched slopes of Italian hills took possession of him. He looked up at George the Greek, dreamily. "Why, say, this stuff, it's got a wonderful taste. Like you said, you got to take it slow, and taste it going down. . . . Have another—and fill mine up. Hamburgers go good with this. Fry me another, will you, George. Onions."

"What 'll your girl say, onions?"

Tony let a half glass of the golden bubbling liquid slide down his throat. He drew in his breath. He drank the remaining half. George filled his glass from the great bottle, three quarters empty now. "She's got nothing to say," Tony announced. "Only what I tell her."

"That's the way. Treat 'em rough right from the start. They like it."

"Like it or lump it, it's all the same to me. . . . Have another glass, George—and give me one, if you don't mind." He was very polite. He felt fine. He hadn't felt so well in years. Strong, clear-headed, purposeful, carefree, light. It was wonderful. George the

Greek was grinning. Tony looked at him scornfully. "Think I'm drunk, don't you? You're crazy. I was brought up on wine, see? My folks used to give me my glass of wine when I was a baby, right along with 'em. Used to it. Of course," he added as though to be strictly fair and aboveboard, "not like this. Not cha-champage—Bolllll—not like this." He drank his sixth and final tumbler. The bottle was empty. His plate, too, was empty. He stood up, smiling, he fished in his pocket and produced a dollar bill. "Keep the change, George. You're a great guy, George."

He felt marvelous, and the amazing part of it was that he knew he felt marvelous. He felt that he could do anything. He was strong, powerful, potent, happy. He went straight to Iolanda's house, though he had no recollection of how he had got there. The store windows had skimmed by him obligingly, that was all. And there he was. Up the three flights of stairs in the same fluid way, very delightful.

"Well?" demanded Iolanda, seeing him without the big bottle. "Did he take it? How much?"

"Who?"

"Who! Crespi."

"Oh, him. No, he didn't want it. Said it was worth twen—twenny fi' dollars."

"Well, where is it? What did you do with it?"

"Drank it."

Then, for the first time, she looked concentratedly at him. "You—you ain't—you didn't drink that—Tony Marucci, you're drunk! You great big bum you, you dirty little rat, you went and drank that whole twenny-five-dollar bottle of champagne would have paid a whole——"

Still smiling, Tony walked over to her and slapped her smartly on the cheek, a light stinging blow. He saw her face staring at him as her own hand flew to her outraged cheek—her eyes her mouth round as the letter O.

"I'm doing what I please with what is mine, see, and that bottle was gave to me by a friend. Scratching around for money the night before you're getting married, like I was a beggar or something. I'll buy your sheets and curtains off you that you was yapping about. You can go back to work at Blum's. Me, I'm Tony Marucci, see, Assis'ant Foreman of the New York Depar'men' of San—uh—Santion, and I pull down twenny-one hunnerd a year. I'll prolly be head of the whole works someday. I'm going to be boss in this family, see. Get that in your head righ' now, or no wedding."

Iolanda's round eyes, Iolanda's round mouth crinkled now into lines of anguish and woe. Iolanda, the termagant, melted before the ruthlessness of the dominating male, Tony Marucci. "Tony!" she cried, her arms thrown about his neck, her cheek on his, "Tony, I didn't mean it, say you didn't mean what you said, too. Tony, you love me, don't you, Tony? Say it!"

At breakfast Alan Career remembered that he hadn't told them to discontinue Patty's paper. There it lay beside his *Times*. "Dahlia, tell the boy to stop Mrs. Career's morning paper until she gets back." He paged it through, idly. There, on the society page, was a picture of Patty leaning ornamentally against the boat-deck rail. They must have snapped it—the newspapermen—while he was below arranging for their dining-room and deck-chair reservations. Patty smiled out at him, young and chic and triumphant. Among those sailing on the Champlain: Mrs. Alan Career. Mrs. Rutger Oliphant with her prize-winning Bedlington Lambheart II. Rhinelander Coudert . . .

"Riffraff!" said Alan Career distinctly, as Dahlia put his buttered toast before him. Then, at her startled look, "No, not you, Dahlia. Uh, look, I think I'll go to the country over the week end. Get a swim and cool off. As Mrs. Career says, nobody's in town."

TREES DIE AT THE TOP

TREES DIE AT THE TOP

THERE WAS NO doubt about it this time. Old Jared Content was dying. High time, too. He had been almost a century at it. All that vitality, all those millions, could not save him now. He had clung to both long after he had any real use for either, the family thought (privately). The San Francisco newspapers had had his obituary filed away in their morgues for half a century and more. The men who had written it and rewritten it were themselves dead and gone while old Jared lived triumphantly on, grown to fabulous age and rugged grandeur, like one of California's native sequoia trees.

Like all good San Franciscans, he had only contempt for that part of California which lay south of his beloved city. For years relatives and friends and physicians had tried to coax him out of the fogs and cold of Russian Hill to the sun-drenched groves of the lower country. He had resisted them with all the strength of his formidable will. The heady air of San Francisco, its scud and winds and hard rare sun were elixir to him. It was, he said, the most civilized city in the United States, and San Franciscans themselves a race of gods who had vanquished the elements; conquered the desert, harnessed the ocean, wrung gold from the mountains and built their own Olympus on the seven hills.

"Look at 'em!" he had been known to shout, brandishing his arms in the midst of Post Street traffic, to the bewilderment of the throngs of passersby. "Where else do you find men like that! And women like goddesses! Walk like race horses, and cheeks like cream and roses. . . . Don't talk to me about Los Angeles. They're all pulp and thick yellow skin down there, like their damned sour oranges."

When that first blow struck him at ninety-five, depriving him of speech and of locomotion, they had carried him, helpless, to the South. There, by a miracle of sheer will, he had partially regained his powers. They said it was the sun and the solitude (both of which he always had hated). He knew it was his iron determination not to die out of sight of his own golden hills and the Golden Gate spread before his vast bedroom window. Like a figure out of the New Testament he took up his bed and walked. Safely back in his beloved San Francisco, clear-headed and undeceived, he made ready for the second blow which he well knew might be the last. He thought about the family, not sentimentally, but with the same grim detachment with which he surveyed his own approaching end.

They had not come to him. On one pretext or another they had stayed away from what they must have thought to be his deathbed. Eager for him to die and get it over with like those scavenger birds that hover at a distance, wings spread, waiting for the final tremor to cease before they swoop on their prey. Fooled 'em, he thought; but not triumphantly. He had been generous enough with the Content millions but he had had, too, an old-fashioned notion that these offspring of pioneer people should make their own way, partially at least. Well, they had. But his own holdings had pyramided there in the West: mines, banks, real estate. Mansions had gone up where shanties had stood; skyscrapers had mushroomed on the mansion sites. Old Jared had been canny and courageous. To trace the source of those attributes you would have needed to go no farther than a glance at the faded tintypes of his father, Jared Content, and his mother, Tamsen. Hadn't he, a lad of seven, made with them the incredibly courageous journey overland inch by inch in '49?

There were strangely few branches of this dying giant tree. Through almost a century he had seen them wither and fall, and now he, the topmost branch, gnarled and sapless, was about to crash. There was left his widowed daughter, nearing seventy, herself more helpless than he, living in Santa Barbara, renegade San Franciscan that she was. There were two grandsons only; five great-grandchildren. The East had claimed them—Chicago and New York. One by one the family had deserted him so that he was like a lone eagle now in his eyrie on the hill overlooking the bay. Yet their very being had come out of San Francisco. Old Jared had never ceased to be bewildered at their leaving it.

Let them come back to it now, he thought. Let them see what lay between the Atlantic and the Pacific. He had seen it at seven, every step of it, every inch of it; not only that, he had walked a good bit of it on his own sturdy little legs. After almost a century of living that journey remained his clearest memory. His actual will had been made long ago, an amazingly brief and simple document for the disposal of riches so vast. This he would not alter.

"But let them come and get it," he said, "the whole kit and boodle of 'em. Grandchildren and great-grandchildren. Have that a provision of the will. I'll make them see this country, by God, if I have to die to do it."

His speech, once so vigorous, was strangely thick and painful now, but his meaning was as plain as his words were homely and American. So the lawyers wrote it down and he signed it with his own great fist, once so powerful, now grown so reluctant. Let them come back to pay final homage, not to him, but to a continent which they took for granted and to a city which they had flouted.

Two weeks later the second blow struck, paralyzing him almost completely so that he lay like a lightning-struck old sequoia. Still miraculously alive, the muted face wore a look not of defeat but of triumph.

FIRST NIGHT

MRS. JAY CONTENT said she wouldn't fly. Not with the children. Furious at the summons she put it plainly. Frances Content was not a word-mincer at any time. "I don't care whose grandfather, or how nearly dead, and how many millions depend on it—though heaven knows we need them. I won't fly across the continent with the children."

They had just opened the house in Lake Geneva for the summer. Luckily, late in the day though it was, they were able because of Jay's influence to get what even Frances Content considered proper accommodations on the San Francisco Streamliner out of Chicago for that night at six-fifteen. Frances Content prided herself on not being a nagging wife but she allowed herself a decent meed of protest in the few frenzied hours preceding their departure for the West. She unburdened herself as she and Jay and Turkey, the children's nurse, and Katharine her maid plunged into the grim business of packing. Jay was studying neckties, surveying each one with passionate intensity before stowing it reverently in the case.

"I think his mind is gone. I don't want to hurt your feelings, Jay, but really! Dragging little children across a continent for a dying old man's whim. You'd think, wouldn't you, that in a hundred years of living he'd have learned something about life?"

"Not quite a hundred."

"Ninety-five, then. What's the difference! And just to hear his will read while he's alive! I never heard of such a thing. It makes me all creepy. . . . Two thousand miles in this heat. I know they're air-conditioned, but just the same . . . Miss Turck, did they absolutely promise to have the twelve quarts of Grade A certified milk down at the train? I can't have the children drinking that wretched train stuff. . . . We'll reach San Francisco half dead ourselves and he'll probably meet us hale and hearty. He'll live to be one hundred and fifty . . . Jay, for heaven's sake, don't take that red necktie, you know you can't wear red at a f . . . Miss Turck, pack their light sweaters right on top where you can get at them first thing. . . . Yes, it's blazing here but the train's air-cooled and you can get pneumonia and Tam had a little sniffle yesterday . . . if that child's going to develop rose fever . . . Look, Jay, I think it would be a good idea to have Griswold stop in at Tebbett's and pick up some of that wonderful smoked salmon and smoked sturgeon and we could give it to the chief steward to put on ice. Train food is so horrible."

"I like it," said Jay Content. "Planked whitefish and chicken potpie and raisin muffins." He stowed a bottle of rye and a bottle of Scotch in the capacious maw of his pigskin bag. "Stuff you never get at home."

"You wouldn't touch it at home. . . . Katharine, I'll take my Persian lamb sport coat, it's freezing in San Francisco after five. . . . The minute the children and everything are settled on the train I'm going to bed and not get up for twenty-four hours."

"Only takes thirty-six to get there."

"Thirty-six! And I hate the very smell of a train. Honestly, Jay, if we hadn't been so broke these last few years, and all those millions of his, and the children's future to think of I'd just refuse to go at all!"

Jay was big, sandy-haired, ruddy, and as much the American husband as this black-haired gray-eyed Frances was the managing and arrogant American wife. But Jay Content was no worm, and he had his quiet humor.

"That's my brave little pioneer woman," he said, and snapped his bag shut.

"Oh, pioneers!" As Frances said it, it sounded like an epithet.

They made quite an imposing procession this steaming July evening as they crossed the Chicago-Northwestern station platform to their train. Of course, Griswold, the chauffeur, wasn't going along, nor Miss Kennedy, Jay's secretary, but they were there in their last-minute official capacity, and working at it. Turck, with little Tam (Tamsen, after her great-great-grandmother) and Jerry (Jared IV, but too confusing); Katharine, the maid; Mr. and Mrs. Content; and a squad of porters carrying such a variety and profusion of bags, boxes, bundles, tins, cases, and toys as to give the parade the look of a safari on the march.

Miss Turck, Tam, and Jerry had the drawing room. Jay Content's compartment adjoined it. Mrs. Content's was just next to that. Thus protected, she would not hear the children's early-morning clamor. When the doors were open right through, the three little rooms gave the effect of quite a spacious apartment on wheels. Katharine had a lower in the next car. They pulled out at six-fifteen in such a welter of Chicago July heat as to make the train's cooled interior a haven.

Within half an hour they had practically set up housekeeping. Frances Content was a wonderful manager. Everything shipshape. She and Miss Turck and Katharine made short work of it. The children's hats, coats, the garments they would need next day, the sleeping garments for tonight, all were hung in the little clothes cupboard so cleverly set into the room. Mrs. Content's clothes were similarly bestowed. The Persian lamb coat, being bulky, was hung behind the door in the room proper, all swathed in a clean sheet provided by the porter. As the great metal train took curves at high speed the sheeted thing swooped out like a wraith to snatch her. There were the necessary jars and bottles that Mrs. Content needed. Katharine placed these on the glass shelves in the medicine cabinet sunk in the wall. Katharine did a hundred things, but then Mrs. Content was terribly busy, too. She glanced in at her husband to see how he was getting on with his unpacking. "Need any help, dear? I'm up to my ears just now, but later Katharine could——"

But he was deep in the Chicago *Evening News*. "My stuff's all out. Everything I need."

"The children are going to have their supper. They're late."

"I'll be in to see them before they go to bed."

"Turkey's taking them into the diner because he's making up their room. I wish you'd go in and see to them. I'm too exhausted to cope. It always helps to—uh—see the chief steward, and we've got that stuff to put on ice. Tam's never been in a diner before, she may bully Turck into giving her ice cream or something instead of egg and applesauce."

"Bully Turck! Nobody could. Mussolini couldn't!"

but he went. Early though it was, the dining car was crowded. Mr. Wiener, the chief steward, was making a great to-do about pulling out chairs and thrusting menus under people's noses, while the colored waiters, dexterous, flexible, tray-laden, swam in and out of the aisle with the agility of porpoises.

Turck, with Tam beside her and Jerry seated opposite, had a fourth at their table in the person of a large blonde lady in pink. The children were starry-eyed and flushed with excitement. Tam, the seeker after truth, was pointing with a relentless finger and saying with terrible distinctness, "Why is that lady sitting at our table?"

"Sh-sh-sh, Tam. Eat your egg."

"But why is she! I don't like her. Make her go away."

Jay to the rescue. He stood beside the table. "How are you doing, Miss Turck? Children all right?" He turned to the pink blonde, he smiled his winning smile. "I hope they're not annoying you."

She looked up at him. Widower? The white mask of fury was miraculously transformed into dimpled tenderness. "I just love kiddies."

"That's fine. Their mother is tired, so I came in to see how they were getting along."

"Pahdon me, suh, pahdon me, suh." He was obstructing a waiter, fearfully laden.

The mask of hate, stiffened by disillusion, again slipped down over the blonde. "Pity she couldn't spare the time to teach her kids manners, if their nurse can't."

"Look, waiter, see that they get everything they want. Let me speak to the chief steward."

"Chief's busy, suh. Yo' kin'ly step outta the aisle?" A dollar bill thrust into his mauve palm. "Yessah, Cap'n. Ah get'm foh you. Jes' step up the end of the car. Yes*suh!* Mistah Wienah!"

"Are you on to the end of the run?" Jay was taking no chances with Mr. Wiener.

"Yes sir." Mr. Wiener was distrait, what with his duties and his sense of importance. "All the way to 'Frisco."

Ten dollars for Mr. Wiener. "Look, we're in the drawing room and compartments B and C in car 69. The porter's got some stuff to put on ice. All right?"

"Certainly, certainly. Anything. Now, would you

like your dinner here, or served in your drawing room? Would you like to order now?"

"I'll eat here, later. Mrs. Content will probably come in with me when she's rested. Seven-thirty, say."

"Fine. Fine. What's the name? I didn't catch——"

"Content. Jared Content. Chicago."

"Ho! Well! Say! Content! I should think everybody. I'll save a nice table for you and the Madam, seven-thirty. Now then, could I make a couple little suggestions, Mr. Content? We get to Omaha about two in the morning. And there we take on for our special passengers some of the grandest little beef tenderloins you ever sunk a tooth in. Special Omaha prize beef. Sweet," Mr. Wiener assured him earnestly, "as sugar. We serve 'em for breakfast, just to special people, you understand, on hot toast. No bigger than this. Two bites to a piece, about four pieces a portion. The tastiest little breakfast dish you ever ate. Melt in the mouth."

Jay Content swallowed. "That sounds great. Not for Mrs. Content, though. She eats very lightly in the morning."

"Now, at Cheyenne we take on fresh-caught mountain trout hustled down specially for us, caught that morning, we serve 'em for lunch, just about two three dozen altogether, they eat like butter, sauté meunière, lemon parsley, and lyonnaise potatoes. The Madam won't say no to those."

A lot you know about what the Madam will say no to, Jay thought. He waved to Miss Turck and to Tam who had a spoon in her mouth, very far down. Arrived at the vestibule of his car 69 (it was named Winnemucca, he noticed, with some distaste) he stopped and drew a deep breath and lighted a cigarette. The vestibule was fantastically hot in contrast to the cars through which he had passed. It was like the withering breath that came from the open hearth of the Gary steel mills in which so much of his money lay sunk these last seven years. He was enough of a sensualist to welcome the outdoor heat of the vestibule so that he might the more relish the cool of the car. He leaned there, swaying easily with the motion, watching the Illinois prairie landscape flashing by in a torrid July haze. The Old Boy's money must have shrunk with everybody else's. The damned income tax and probably a lot of bad paper. Inheritance tax would take a fierce bite out of it, too. Must be a little cuckoo. Frances probably right. Making them come and watch him die, like royalty. If you failed to show up you were out of the will, eh? Bet you could break a will like that on the grounds of mental incompetence. Magnificent old devil, at that. Across the continent in a covered wagon when he was no more than Jerry's age. Guts, that crowd. Suppose he and Frances and Jerry and Tam . . . Heat dust desert. Oxen. Mountains. He looked out at the shimmering farm lands, exhaled, dropped his cigarette and carefully stepped on it. As he entered 69 the cool air was as refreshing as water to one thirsty.

Frances was standing before the mirror in his compartment, creaming her face. She looked lovely as a Benda mask with all that smear of white, and her dark smooth hair and deep-set gray eyes. The porter, aided by Katharine, was making up her room for the night, though outside was brilliant summer daylight.

"What in the world, Jay! I thought you were never coming back. Are they all right?"

"Sure. They're seeing life. Good for 'em. The chief steward said he'd have a table for us. Oh, damn, I forgot to tell him to send me a bottle of water. Heh, porter! Bottle of water. How about a little drinkie, Mrs. C., before dinner?"

"I wouldn't go in to dinner tonight," said Mrs. C., patting cream, "if I were starving to death. I may get up for dinner tomorrow night, if I feel rested. I'm having my dinner in bed."

"Oh. Well." He was disappointed. He hated eating alone. "How about ordering, then? I'll tell them. What do you want?"

"I'll have a tiny highball with you before you go in. Just cold chicken—white meat—and chicory salad. Tell them oil lemon ice and a bowl. Katharine will mix it, their dressing is always foul. I might have some cream cheese and a jar of Bar-le-Duc, with salt wafers. Katharine will heat me some milk at ten."

Katharine now knocked discreetly at the open door. "It's all made up, madam." Frances, still patting, passed into her own room. Scotch or rye, said Jay, in the doorway. Her room was indeed made up. The drab Pullman bed had become a couch of luxury. Her own pale peach crepe de Chine sheets scenting the air delicately with heliotrope; a nest of peach pillows, hemstitched; her own satin-edged summer-weight blanket neatly sheathed in a silk slip; her plainest little tailored bed jacket laid out.

The children were coming along the corridor. Tam was squealing, Jerry was roaring, Miss Turck was saying Children Children in her clipped Canadian accents. "Oh, dear, they're on the rampage. I knew it." Frances tied tighter the cord of her robe and prepared to do battle in the drawing room. She passed through Jay's room into theirs. Jay was mixing the highballs and whistling softly between his teeth.

"Let Turkey wrestle with them."

The unwonted excitement, the unusual hours, had got them completely out of hand. They bounced on the beds, they splashed water, pressed push buttons, turned on the electric fan, yelled. Tam suddenly remembered a dreadful dismembered doll which she always took to bed with her, and whose mangled remains had been forgotten in the rush of packing. She now set up a keening that could be heard in the next car. Turck gathered her up.

"Just let me cope, Mrs. Content. I'll quiet them. Not so many people is better. . . . Sh-sh . . . Look, she's asleep." Tam had indeed gone off in the middle of a sob. "Jerry, you haven't brushed your teeth. See, you're to sleep up there, and a little fence thing to keep from falling out . . . No, it isn't a baby crib. Nothing of the kind. Only big boys can sleep way up there." A tower of strength, Miss Turck; fortyish, neat blue-gray uniforms, sensible flat oxfords with rubber heels, broad flat fingernails with little white flecks in them; a bosom flat, too, and composed of some wooden material like a Japanese pillow, unyielding; fine on formulae; Jerry and Tam were exactly the proper weight for their years.

"Oh-o-o-o-o!" breathed Mrs. Content, closing the drawing room door behind her, thus shutting it off from Jay's room. "No," as he offered her a frosty glass, "not here. I'm going to get into bed first. Bring it to me, dear. I'm exhausted. Simply sunk."

"How about a bite of that smoked salmon with your highball? I'll tell the steward. It'll give you an appetite for your chicken, later."

He saw her settled among her pillows with her book and a bottle of fresh-smelling toilet water and a mild highball. The little room, cool, perfumed, had actually taken on an air of elegance.

"Well, Fran, I think I'll go in and have my dinner." He glanced about the compartment. "Got everything you want?" The American husband, hugging his chains. "The waiter will be along with your tray any minute now. I've got the chief steward all buttered up."

By the time he had finished dinner it was nearly nine, but the western sky was still aglow. Luckily he had met two men he knew. The three had dined together and had sat smoking and talking for an hour after that in the club car. The radio was on and they heard the late evening news from Chicago and New York. There was among the passengers a table or two of bridge. Others were deep in books or magazines. Jay Content was pleasantly tired but not sleepy. The thought of his own bedroom did not appeal to him; stuffy; and besides, no place to sit, and Frances probably asleep. He'd turn in at eleven and read for an hour or so. It was agreeable talking about business, Roosevelt, Europe, recovery, taxes, politics, golf. At eleven they broke up. Well, mighty nice running into you like this. . . . See you tomorrow. . . . Might have a little bridge. . . . How long you going to be in 'Frisco, Jay?

. . . Well, hard to say. Not long. My grandfather's very sick, dying, in fact. . . . Well, say, I'm sorry to hear that. Lives out there, does he? . . . Oh, yes, he's an old settler. Crossed the country with his parents in a covered wagon when he was a kid. They were Forty-Niners, you know, my great-grandparents. . . . Is that right! Well, great stock, that bunch. Yessir, it took guts. . . . Well, see you tomorrow.

The door between his room and hers was open, her lights were on. "Jay! Jay, we've had the most awful time with Jerry. I was going to send for you, and then I hated—— He won't go to sleep, he's keeping Tam awake, Turck can't do a thing with him, it's over-excitement, he keeps hanging his head over the edge of the berth, if the train lurches he'll dash out his brains——"

The drawing room was a shambles. Even Miss Turck had a wild look. The boy's eyes were at once brilliant and heavy, his black hair stood on end, his legs were in the air and he was enjoying the novelty of paddling his bare feet against the car ceiling from the vantage point of the upper berth. He was balancing on his head to do so.

Jay Content gathered the boy up, blanket and all. "Come on, son. We menfolks will go off by ourselves a little while, shall we?"

"Jay, what——?" she called from her room as he entered his.

He closed the drawing room door behind him, leaving Turck and Tam in peace. "Go to sleep, France. Never mind, we're all right. I'll attend to this. You go to sleep." He shut the door between his room and hers, he laid the boy on the bed, and covered him. He took off his suit coat, got into his dressing gown and lay down beside him, cozily. "Let's talk. What'll we talk about, son?"

"Indians."

"Indians!"

"That lady at supper, the one at our table, said everything around here used to be Indians, they were all the way to California, they used to sneak up at night and cut the tops of people's heads off with the hair on and wear it, and they shot arrows with poison on the end and you died."

"She did, eh? Well, a lot of the Indians were pretty decent, considering what the white people did to them. Your great-grandfather that we're going to San Francisco to see was just about your age when he went from Illinois to California. His father and mother took him and his little sister. His father's name was Jared Content, like yours, and his mother's name was Tamsen, like Tam's. We keep on naming people Jared and Tamsen in our family. That was almost a hundred years ago, before there was a railroad or anything. Come to think of it, they made almost the same trip that you and Mother and Tam and I are making now, only they didn't have soft beds to sleep in, and waiters and cooks and electric lights and hot water. It took them three months."

"Will it take us three months?"

"No, son. We'll be there day after tomorrow. They traveled all the way, over prairie and desert and mountains in a prairie schooner."

"What's a prairie schooner? You're fooling. I know a schooner's a boat, you can't go over mountains in a boat."

"This wasn't a boat, it was a big wagon. They called it a prairie schooner because the top of the wagon was canvas and it made a kind of round tent . . ."

FIRST MONTH

THE TOP of the wagon was canvas and made a kind of round tent. There were scores of them drawn up here at Independence, Missouri. They billowed white against the prairie horizon like waves of the ocean. Not that she had ever seen an ocean. Here they were, bound for the Pacific, but she didn't want to see it. The little creek that ran through the farm back home in Illinois was ocean enough for Tamsen Content. Jared had told her that Independence, Missouri, was the real start of the trip to California. She knew now what he had meant. All these wagons drawn up, ready for the start in the morning, their white canvas tops like a fleet of schooners. Of course, that was why they called them prairie schooners, she said to herself, rather foolishly. When morning had come she sat tight-lipped and staring hard to keep from crying. Jared picked up the reins and the ox-goad, shouted to the oxen, they gathered themselves together, their great flanks moved, their muscles rippled beneath the brown hide. Jared's mare was tied and following behind. And the wagon with the supplies was behind theirs. Jacob, the hired man, and Lavina, the hired girl, had charge of that. They had married, conveniently, before starting. Jarry was back there with them. She could hear him whooping and shouting to the oxen. The milch cow, faithful Velvet, was tied behind their wagon—Velvet because of her eyes and because of the richness of her creamy milk. There was a third supply wagon, but the Contents had only a half interest in that. They shared it with their erstwhile neighbors back in Illinois, now their traveling companions to California, the Haskins, Ambrose and Sarah.

Little Tam lay asleep in her arms, up there on the wagon seat, perched so high. "You can't hold her like that all the way to California," Jared said. "From May to August. She's a big girl. Three years and past."

"I know. But she didn't get her sleep out, up before daybreak for this early start. Look, the sun's just coming up now. It's going to be fair. That's a good sign, isn't it, Jared?"

"That left hind wheel's squeaking again, before we're rightly started. And I paid that wheelwright two bits at Independence, like a fool."

She looked down at the child's face, rosy in the folds of her shawl, the sunrise flushing it pinker. "It was all a pother, back there. Nobody closed an eye last night, I'll be bound. We're well away from it, only——"

She left the sentence unfinished. For a moment her mind held the picture of last night's vigil. May in Missouri, the night was sharp but not too cold. They had slept in the wagons, of course; Jared and Tamsen in the big wagon, with Jarry and Tam. Jacob and Lavina in the other. Tamsen never lay down in the wagon that she did not think of her four-post bed with the calico valance and the candlewick spread she herself had made. It was all there in the second wagon, with the other household goods, tied and wrapped. How luxurious it seemed! When would she sleep in it again? The stars had been brilliant last night. Millions of them, big and blue-white like the diamond she had seen in the brooch worn by Mrs. Squire Reade, back home. Back home. The safe little farm back there in Illinois. But Jared had the roving spirit, his people had come to Illinois from Connecticut, and before that to Connecticut from England. Besides, the Illinois winters had not agreed with him. He coughed, and his cheeks had hollow places in them so that his long Anglo-Saxon head looked longer. He had heard the stories of this California of gold and sunshine. People were flocking there from all over Illinois and Missouri and even back East. Jared did not talk much. But once his mind was made up it was no use. She had learned that.

Last night had been torture. No matter how far they had come before, Independence, Missouri, was the starting place, the jumping-off place. Once well out of it, there was no turning back. The camp was in a jitter of nerves and anticipation. It seemed no one slept. From sunset to dawn there were sounds. Lanterns flashing. The stamp of hooves—oxen, mules, horses. The long bray of a mule, a horse's whinny. A shout of laughter. Someone singing. Drunk, probably.

"When you start for San Francisco,
They treat you like a dog,
The victuals you're compelled to eat
Ain't fit to feed a hog."

The slap-slap of cards. A whimper of fear from the recesses of some dark wagon. An old man with his family around a late campfire, his bearded patriarchal face, his hollow voice uplifted in supplication: Whither shall I go from thy spirit? Whither shall I flee from thy presence? If I ascend up into heaven, thou art there. If I make my bed in hell, behold, thou art there. If I take the wings of the morning, even there thy hand shall lead me . . . Whee-yip! Ee-yow! Roisterers; or cow hands, maybe. The night had seemed endless, but the dawn had come too soon.

"Only what?" Jared said, to her unfinished sentence. She came out of her thoughts with a start. Stared. "Only what?" he insisted, rather testily, for him.

"Nothing, really. I was just thinking—I mean—once you're well away from Independence, Missouri, why, there's no turning back, ever."

"I should think not! Every stick and stone and dollar we possess is right here in these wagons. Turn back indeed!"

How many times, in the months that followed, she thought of that first morning out of Independence. They were a small wagon train, as California-bound parties counted in that day. Twenty-five wagons. The Contents owned two of these and half of another. Their world was contained therein. Her most precious belongings; her sheet-iron stove, her feather beds and pillows, pots, kettles, her precious willow-pattern dishes, her four-poster bed, her cherished walnut table (that made awkward luggage indeed), her dresses and the children's, in trunks; her little box of water colors and her brushes, for she loved to sketch; she had even brought books, this Tamsen Content, who had been briefly the pretty schoolmistress of the district school before she had married Jared. As for Jared, his luggage was sterner stuff: an anvil and bellows, crowbar, auger, ax, chisel, harness, kegs. Jacob, the hired man, had brought his accordion. Then there were, of course, hundreds of pounds of flour, besides ham, bacon, sugar, coffee, tea, cream of tartar, soda, salt, dried fruit, beans, rice, pilot bread, pepper, ginger, tartaric acid. They well knew what to take along. Jared wasn't long-headed for nothing. So they traveled that first month—farmers, lawyers, merchants, preachers, laborers. As Tamsen, last night, had fitfully dreamed of the Illinois farm, so they had dreamed of their Vermont hills, their Kentucky fields, the lakes of Maine, the Massachusetts woodlands, the Indiana prairies. Gold! Adventure! Twenty-two hundred miles lay before them.

At the conclave held by every member of the wagon train on the second day out they had offered Jared Content the captaincy, but he had refused. "An older wiser head for captain," he had said. "Let me be lieutenant, like. Besides, I'm subject to little spells of feeling poorly, and might fail you in a pinch. I thank you for the honor, folks. If I could make a suggestion I'd say Ambrose Haskins for captain, he is a neighbor of mine back in Illinois—was, I should say—and can turn his hand to anything, with a wise head to guide it, and us."

Ambrose, elected, had risen and had spoken briefly, grimly. "Folks, neighbors, fellow travelers, we've got twenty-two hundred miles to go to Hangtown, Californy. Between here and there we got a sight of high mountains, broad desert, great rivers and hostile Indians. But it ain't those that 'll give us most grief. You can figger it out for yourself. May, June, July, part of August; about one hundred twenty days. How much a day, every cussed day, rain or shine, hail, cholera, breakdowns, floods, dust storms, washouts, lost critters? . . . That's right, folks. Above eighteen miles a day. Eighteen miles a day, no matter what, or you get stuck in the autumn snows on the High Sierras and eat each other like the Donner party done, in '46."

A scream from one of the women. The rest, white-faced, turned to look at her in disapproving silence.

Still, that first month wasn't so bad, Tamsen thought, as June came on them. May in Missouri, in Kansas, in Nebraska; winding their slow dogged way across the prairies and the plains. She was surprised to find that the prairies had knolls and even hills. She always had thought they were flat like the farm land back home. Why, they had talked of the California Trail as though it were a plainly marked wagon road. But on the high plateaus there was never a wagon track at all; the wind covered with dust and sand every boot or wheel track an hour after it was made. The wind! Tamsen looked ruefully at her face and neck and arms and hands and hair. The sun and the wind and the dust had wrought their will on them. A farm woman, inured to manual labor, used to battling with the elements, eight years a wife, she still had kept her pretty ways, she prided herself on her clear creamy skin, her slender hands, shapely in spite of the drudgery. But this was different. There was no fighting this.

They crossed the Kansas River, the widest stream they would encounter in the whole twenty-two hundred miles. "But not the trickiest," old uncle Bob McGlashan said. "Wait till you git to the Platte. Three feet deep, mebbe, but a current kin sweep ye, oxen and all, to the bottom of a mud trap, and gone. She flows bottom side up, old Platte does."

You got used to it. You learned a kind of oriental patience. Tamsen recalled with amusement how irked they had been at having to wait their turn seven hours in order to ferry across the Kaw. Heat and dust. Men and women, horses mules oxen, tortured by enormous venomous flies. That had been the first week in May. It seemed nothing now. Past graves, marked with an elk horn, for wood was too precious to be used thus. Bones of animals whitening on the plains. Broken-down outfits bogged near the Big Blue, trapped in the rich wet spring soil of eastern Kansas.

By the end of May certain things stood out stark

and clear, good and bad. They kept track of the days, she and Jared. One month had gone. The children were well, though thinnish. Velvet's milk was not what it had been. Jared was well—that is, you might say, well enough. He'd always had those hollows in the cheeks. Not dark like that, though, Tamsen thought, as if dirty fingers had smeared beneath the cheekbones.

The evening of May 31st they took stock of the month past as they sat around the campfire after supper. Bacon, beans, bread. Abiah Pinney, who knew the route, having once before gone beyond the Sweetwater, said they soon would have fresh meat in plenty —or should. Antelope and buffalo meat. Buffalo hump, Abiah vowed, was the sweetest eating meat there was. Tamsen thought it sounded fairly sickening. She envisioned a plump frying chicken with hot biscuits and cream gravy for Jared and the children; such food as they had not known since they left the farm. She must not think of such things, it was greedy. Besides, hadn't Lavina baked an apple pie tonight as a special treat, to celebrate the first month passed? Dried fruit, of course, but delicious, with a little of Velvet's scant cream poured over each portion.

At home on the farm she had prided herself on having kept things "nice" in the household. A checked tablecloth even at breakfast instead of the oilcloth of the average farm kitchen; napkins to match; the butter kept firm and sweet in the cold spring water; red geraniums in the kitchen window. Now their table was the ground, their tablecloth a piece of rubber which was used as a cloak when it rained. Dishes of tin, spoons of iron. At first it had been like a picnic, but the novelty had long worn off. Even the children felt the discomfort of sitting cross-legged on the ground three times a day, and they refused to eat the coarse stuff called mountain bread, which was simply flour and water mixed and fried in grease. She tried not to think of the angel cake for which she had been famous in the countryside. The whites of a dozen new-laid eggs went into it. It was sweet and light and melted like snow on the tongue.

"End of the first week in June," Abiah Pinney was saying, "with any luck, that is, we ought to be in Fort Laramie, Wyoming."

Wyoming! thought Tamsen, what a wild-sounding place. She, Tamsen Hoyt Content, with Jared and

Jarry and little Tam—what were they doing headed for a place called Wyoming? Around the next campfire they were singing in chorus, pleasant to hear, though some of the songs were too rough for her taste.

"Hangtown gals are plump and rosy,
Hair in ringlets mighty cozy;
Painted cheeks and gassy bonnets,
Touch them and they'll sting like ho'nets."

She liked better such songs as *Auld Lang Syne* and *Bonnie Charlie* and *I Remember, I Remember.* Or *Oh, Susanna* with its heartening chorus:

"Oh, Susanna, oh, don't you cry for me,
I've come from Alabama, wid my banjo on my knee."

"Last week in June," Abiah went on, "we should by rights reach the South Pass, summit of the Rockies and the Continental Divide."

"The Rocky Mountains!" Lavina exclaimed, rather incredulously, as though she had not expected this. Lavina had only such book-learning as Tamsen, her mistress, had been able to give her at odd moments when the farmhouse work was done.

"Certainly, girl, certainly. Did you expect to git to Californy without noticing the Rocky Mountains!" Abiah said humorously.

"South Pass they'll need their songs," Ambrose Haskins predicted grimly. He nodded toward the singing campfire group. "That is, if they can spare the breath to sing 'em."

Tam and Jarry were supposed to be sound asleep in the wagon. The singing must have wakened them. Tamsen saw their tousled heads poking out of the canvas flap. "Tam! Jared Content! Get back to bed this minute!" They grinned impishly in the firelight and did not budge. They were getting out of hand with this rough life, living like gypsies. Tomorrow she'd start lessons, though it wasn't easy now that she was doing part of the driving each day when Jared began to look too queer and drawn. It wasn't driving. You walked along by the side of the oxen in the blazing sun and the wind. Sometimes you could rest a brief while up in the wagon seat. But they were stupid creatures, the oxen, and had to be guided and prodded. The mule-drawn wagons seemed to get on faster. She wished Jared hadn't been so set on oxen.

"Time will come," Jared was saying gravely, "when they'll have a railway all the way from New York State to Californy. I predict it, and soon."

"Yah!" hooted Jacob, the hired man, who had grown very free. "And git mule teams to haul the enjines over the mountains!"

Lavina tittered at her husband's wit.

But Uncle Bob McGlashan nodded his grizzly head sagely, in agreement with Jared. "There are wonders to come never dreamt of on land or sea. I say with Jared here the day will come they'll make the trip by railway in three weeks."

Tamsen looked about her proudly. "Jared's right, likely. Jared's always right. But they'll never see what we've seen, this trip. Not rushing along like that, they won't."

Sarah Haskins looked up from her knitting. "I was thinking today, the sights we've seen this past month, and the strange things have happened. Things I'll never forget, not if I live to be a hundred. The man who cut his horses free midstream in the current to save them, and he on the back of one of them, and let his wife and children in the wagon bed float downstream to their death if it hadn't been for Abiah and Uncle Bob catching hold of it at the narrow bend in the stream. Never will I forget the poor wife's face, and the screams of the little ones."

"Dirtier skunk never drew breath," agreed Uncle Bob. "I pity the outfit he's traveling with. Our boys were for stringing him up from a wagon tongue if Ambrose here hadn't stopped 'em. I reckon he figgered wives come cheap but horses is worth their weight in gold in Californy."

Lavina snuggled closer to her Jacob. "I keep thinking, nights, of those first Indians we saw when we was along the Little Blue. Pawnees, wasn't they, Jacob? How they rode along on their ponies looking neither to right or left, over two hundred of them, it froze me to the bone. Nobody can't make me believe they are friendly. Red devils!"

"That child," Tamsen said, almost in a whisper, "that had splintered his leg and they'd never set it and it began to gangrene and how they tried finally to cut it off and he——" She shuddered and buried her face in her hands.

They all chimed in, then. . . . The man who'd

traveled seven hundred miles and turned back because his mother-in-law made him, she said she'd made a living before she ever heard of Californy. . . . The man who drank too much cold water at Alcove Spring, poor feller, to die of that. . . . The coffin they made for that Mormon widow's man, out of pieces of their own precious wagon beds. . . . The groves of wild plum trees on the Little Blue, where they had camped amidst loveliness, and the terrible downpour at dawn so that they found themselves camped in a lake at daybreak. And the call of a humorous camp sentry at the waking hour: "Five o'clock and all is wet!"

"Well," said Tamsen, "it's bedtime. Coming, Jared?"

Sarah Haskins neatly rolled her knitting. "I never thought to see the day—night, rather—when I could lay my bones down on a wagon bed mattress week on week and sleep sound. It just shows."

"Doesn't it!" Tamsen agreed brightly. She put her hand on Jared's shoulder, he slipped his arm around her.

"No fair for married couples spoonin'," yelled Uncle Bob McGlashan.

FIRST DAY

IT SEEMED to Jay Content that for hours he had been feverishly aware of the children's early-morning clamor and Turck's unavailing efforts to quiet them. "But he never sleeps this late, Turkey. He gets up and goes to the office. I want to see him shaving."

"He isn't going to the office. He's on a train. Now hush, Jerry, do. It was you kept him and all of us awake till midnight, and after. It was well past that when he brought you back to your own bed, like a great baby."

"Don't you call me a baby. I'll tell my father."

"Do."

Tam's voice. "I want to see Mummy."

"Mummy's sleeping."

"I want a cooky. I'm hungry."

"Likely story, this time of morning, a cooky. Besides, you had your breakfast only an hour ago."

Haggard, groaning, Jay looked at his watch. Half-past nine! Well, I must have had some sleep, after all. That damned racket at Omaha, just as I was dropping off. Omaha. Oma—those little steaks. Don't feel quite up to steaks, after telling bedtime stories until all hours. Still, maybe a shower and shave—no, I guess I'll have the train barber give me a shave after breakfast. Ten o'clock before I get in to breakfast as it is.

He listened at her door, he opened it cautiously and peered in. The room was dim, silent. He sneaked down the corridor, he had a refreshing shower, hot and cold. When he returned the children fell on him, but he silenced them with promises and threats.

"No, you can't come into breakfast with me. I want you to stay in your room, with the door shut, so that you won't wake Mother. If you are good and quiet I'll have lunch with you, we'll all eat together in the dining car. Oh, God, I won't be able to eat mountain trout at 12.30 when I'm having breakfast steaks at 10.30—well, anyway, I'll sit with you."

"May we have ice cream for lunch?"

"Yes." Rashly. Miss Turck cast him a reproachful look.

"A certain young person has a tiny little c, o, l, d."

"Pooh, I know what that spells," Jerry announced. "It spells cold. Tam's got a cold, she prolly can't have any ice cream."

Tam opened her mouth to scream, Turck said, yes you can too lovey but come here and let Turkey put drops up your nose.

"I won't."

"Why don't you take them back to the lounge car and let them listen to the radio, Miss Turck? Lots of magazines with pictures, too."

Miss Turck's features took on a British glaze before his very eyes. "Please, Mr. Content. Tam mustn't have a change of room temperature—it's bad enough in here, this cold-air system. Besides, they've their own books and toys—dozens of them."

But the damage had been done. "We want to go to the lounge car. Daddy said we could. I want to listen to the radio. You're not the boss of us. Daddy said we could. He said it himself."

Jay Content fled to the dining car and the undesired and promised bits of tenderloin steak that would melt in the mouth.

It was, somehow, eleven before he had dealt with

the beef and Mr. Wiener and the strange morning paper which, like all train newspapers picked up en route, seemed to have column after column of nothing in it. When he returned to his compartment it was made up and tidied for the day. The children's room looked like a State Street toy shop at Christmas. Mechanical sets, dolls, books, games. Tam, somewhat smeared, was busy with paper, a brush, and water colors in a precarious state.

"She's making a lovely water-color painting for her mummy when she wakes up, aren't you, ducky?" Turck said, and rescued the red just in time.

"Let her say it herself," Jay found himself snapping at her, to his own surprise.

"She's only three, after all," Miss Turck said, defending her darling as though he had accused her of crime.

"If she's old enough to use water colors on a train she's old enough to say so for herself." What was he talking about, he thought. Those steaks must have disagreed with him. Too heavy and rich for breakfast. Miaowing at Turkey like an old she-cat.

He heard Katharine's voice in compartment C.

Then Frances was awake. He knocked, he opened the door between his room and hers. "Hello! How'd you sleep?"

"Sleep! Look, darling, don't come in, this place is a shambles, three people in here would call for a traffic cop. How are the children, tell Turck to come here a minute. I didn't close an eye all night. Not an eye. I look like Dracula."

"How about breakfast?"

"Katharine rang. I'm just having orange juice and black coffee."

"Well, I guess I'll go to the barber shop and get a shave. If you think you look like Dracula you ought to see me as Tarzan."

When he returned Frances was sitting up in bed among her rosy pillows, looking fresh and cool and young. She had on a bed jacket with a pattern of tiny sprigged flowers, quaint and fetching. The little room had a refreshing woodsy smell, Frances' kiss was delicately scented, her dark hair was fragrant and soft and neat, her gray eyes clear; her little stack of books on the shelf above her head, her needlework bag at her feet, her smart traveling clock on the windowsill, her robe folded at the foot of the bed, she was jotting things down in a small blue leather notebook. Frances always made orderly little notes in bed, night and morning, under a list entitled Things To Do. Cryptic notes. tel upholst. extra man try Winky. send blue cleanr. Tam drops. brdg lamp.

"Had breakfast?"

"The orange juice was warm and the coffee cold. Wouldn't you think, on a train that's supposed to be good—and last night they stopped somewhere for hours and hours and people outside yelled to each other, all named Bill, no wonder it takes thirty-six hours."

"Well, they have to do something about ice and food and fuel, you know, like any household."

"What in the world were you talking to Jerry about last night! You rumbled on and on; that's no way to quiet a child. What were you saying?"

"Oh, I was telling him the yarn about the way Grandfather and his folks made the trip in '49. I told him it was almost exactly the same route we're taking on this train. He was interested."

She glanced idly out at the Western landscape. "Was it? Where are we? Look, darling, Tam drew me a picture in water colors, isn't it touching! It seems it is supposed to be a house."

"How about getting up for lunch? Come on, be a sport. Fresh trout."

"I simply couldn't. Do be sweet about it, Jay. I'll get up for dinner tonight, I promise."

He went into the dining car with the children and Turck at twelve-thirty, but he did not eat. He watched them and approved as they ate their vegetables. Ice cream, yes, but you've got to drink your milk. Their special certified milk was brought them, each bottle dated like vintage wine. Replete, they were brought into their mother's room before their nap. Frances was stitching on her tapestry, an ambitious work intended for a chair covering, on which she had been sewing, like a medieval princess, for a year or more. The wools were green and gold and deep red and cathedral blue, a delicious melange of color. Tam loved to play with them, though it was forbidden.

Tam, the precocious, regarded her recumbent parent with the merciless steady stare of the very young. She and Jerry knew about breakfast-in-bed-for-Mother. But this was afternoon; and on a train.

"Why are you in bed, Mummy?"

"Because Mother's tired, sweetie."

"Why?"

"She had to work so hard to get everything ready for all of us on this trip."

"Why?"

"So that you and Jerry and Daddy would be comfortable."

"Why?"

Frances discarded the sweetly maternal tone and all her child psychology training. She sat bolt upright. Her voice rang above the roar of the train. "Turkey! Miss Turck! Come and get Tam. She's driving me crazy. Anyway, it's time for their nap."

"I'm too big for naps," Jerry announced. "I'm never going to nap again, 'specially on a train."

Turck came in crisp and capable and Turck thought not. "No nap? And you've been up half the night and keeping everybody else awake. You'll pop right off. Come along." Turkey's large-knuckled hand closed over Tam's soft pink fingers like a cactus pad on a rose.

"Anyway I'm sick of this old train," Jerry shouted.

"Hush. Come along, there's a good boy and I've a treat for you."

"What? What kind of a treat? I don't believe it."

"Your father says we come to a place called Ogden-utah at half-past four, it's quite a large city I believe, we stay ten minutes, you may walk out on the platform, you and Tam, if you're both good and take your naps; and we'll buy picture postcards. So now!"

"Oh, pooh, old picture postcards!" Tam, slave and adorer of her brother, found this an arresting phrase and now echoed it as best she could as the two were gently hustled off. It came out pitty potard or some such matter, but the boredom in her tone was a triumph of slavish imitation.

Frances' needle plunged in and out of the tapestry stretched tightly over the frame. It made a popping sound.

Jay stuck his head in at the door. "I'm going to have lunch with some fellows I met. One of them is that young Murchison who's with the Flint people. I've been trying to get at him for a couple of years. It's a break, meeting him like this on the train. Look, Fran, do something for me, will you?"

"Within reason. But no bringing him in for a chat and a drink. I'm no Du Barry."

"His wife's on the train, and their little girl. She isn't well—Mrs. Murchison, I mean—and she has to spend the winter in Tucson. He says it's bronchial, but sounds like lungs to me. They've got a section three cars back. Murchison hasn't any money—the Flint people don't pay him enough, he's worth twice his salary to me if I can persuade him to—look, go back and talk to her, will you? She's spending a week in San Francisco with him before she goes to Tucson. We'll ask them to have dinner with us there, but I'd like to get going with him right now. Will you do that, honey?"

But over honey's face there slipped the icy mask of negation. He knew it well. "Darling, dinner in San Francisco, yes—if you think that business dinners and deathbeds go well together. But please don't ask me to be the hostess and the little woman today."

"I just thought if you were getting up, why——"

"But I'm not. And Tam's got a cold already. I won't have her playing with strange train children."

"All right. Forget I ever brought it up. Aren't you going to have some lunch?"

"Later perhaps. I'm not hungry now. Run along, dear." She smiled tolerantly. "Tell the porter to send Katharine to me." She ceased her stitching and lay back a moment, her eyes shut. There was a discreet knock at the door. Katharine, in neat black, came to her bedside. "Katharine, see if there's a manicure on this train. There must be. My nails are frightful. I didn't have time, rushing off this way. I think she'd better do it—rather than you, I mean—because she's probably used to the train lurching, and all. Tell her I'll want her at about half-past two. And get out my own polish. Their stuff is awful. At three order me a grilled sardine sandwich on whole-wheat toast and half a grapefruit. And tell them for heaven's sake the sandwich hot and the grapefruit cold."

Katharine closed the door softly behind her. They were slowing down a little as they approached a town. Frances glanced out to view the burning Western landscape. A Chamber of Commerce sign said Welcome To Green River Wyoming. A little station came into sight with yokels standing on the platform gaping at the train. Frances pulled down her window shade. She lay back in her little nest of cool pink crepe and closed her eyes. Welcome To Green River Wyoming. She shuddered. People actually lived here. The train came to the briefest stop. In another moment they were moving. Again the luxury train cleft the continent.

SECOND MONTH

JARED HAD TRADED some of his oxen for mules—his beautiful costly oxen for these vulgar little beasts. But at Fort Laramie they had told him that he'd never make the mountain passes without mules. Oxen were all right for the plains, they said, but mules for the mountains. Besides, not so much feed and water. These Midwestern farmers had no knowledge of mountain and desert. They knew about crops, about the four seasons, woods, water, weather, animals of their own section of the vast continent. But Western trail signs, canyons, deserts, arroyas; Indians, buffalo; blazing hot days followed by freezing nights; these things were new, bewildering. They had no knowledge to cope with these.

It was queer how you took for granted—and even found commonplace, finally—things which you had never expected to see or experience. That first vast herd of buffalo. Abiah Pinney, with his superior knowledge of the plains, had been the first to spy them. Riding his mare Nancy ahead of the wagon train, as he often did, he had suddenly wheeled and ridden back at high speed, one arm, with its pointing finger, waving frantically toward a black spot on the horizon. The black spot moved, grew larger, came nearer.

"Buff'lo!" he yelled. "They must be millions of them coming up from the river. Turn your teams around so you're headin' with the herd, and hold on to your critters, and keep your young'uns in the wagons." On they swept, thundering nearer and nearer, a river, a sea of buffalo. You heard the rifles crack in every direction, some of the men were shooting from their horses, others from the wagons in which they sat. The herds swept on and on, running between the wagons like flowing water. The mules danced and snorted.

"Buffalo meat for supper and till kingdom come, looks like," Jared said.

That night Tamsen looked up from her plate of

broiled buffalo hump. The air of distaste with which she had at first regarded it had vanished. "Why, it's good! It's delicious!" Abiah Pinney, his mouth full, munched and nodded with an air of I-told-you-so.

Jared and Tamsen agreed that everything seemed suddenly to change after they had left Fort Laramie. You felt it once you had left the adobe walls of the Fort, situated there near the Oglala and Brûlé divisions of the Sioux nation and not far from the tribes of the Cheyennes and Arapahoes. The sky seemed vaster as the horizon broadened. The men of the party looked to their axes, their shovels and crowbars. Serious, even grave, they said it was heavy going from now on, with the Black Hills just ahead of them. The trail became rougher; there were steep hills for the first time—so steep that the women and children got out and slid down as best they could, holding on here and there to a rock or a bit of brush to check their slipping feet. By now Tamsen and Jared and even Jarry and little Tam often walked to save their bones the hideous jolting of the wagon over the ruts. They had learned to sway with the motion of the schooner, but sometimes when she lay down to rest at night it seemed to

Tamsen that every bone in her body was broken. She and Jared drove turn and turn about now. Jared would walk, or ride his mare or even lie resting in the back of the wagon. Tamsen pretended not to think it strange that Jared should be lying down in the daytime.

They began to pass queer objects by the trail side. Bleaching bones they were used to; camp refuse, carcasses of dead animals, even an occasional broken wagon-wheel rim. But now, suddenly, as the way became rougher, steeper, deeper in dust, they came upon articles once thought invaluable, now abandoned. Large blacksmiths' anvils, plows, grindstones, harness, cooking stoves; even clothing and bacon and beans, thrown out by wagon trains that had gone before.

Jared stared at these, then he turned to look down at Tamsen seated there beside him. "Overloaded." Something in his tone made her stare at him, but he was looking straight ahead now, his young face set and stern. "So are we. Ambrose and Pinney both said we most of us are. Overloaded. Iron stuff. Crockery. That big walnut bedstead."

"No!" cried Tamsen. "I won't let you. I'll get out

and carry it myself. No, not my four-poster that I've thought about a thousand times! Jared Content, it's for our new house in California! What does he know! What does that Ambrose Haskins know, more than we do! Let Sarah throw away her——"

"She's a-going to," Jared interrupted quietly. "So're you, Tamsen. There's no way out, if we want to reach Californy before snowfall."

But before the end of June she could look back at this and wonder that she had ever considered it important, or even worth a second thought. By the end of June Velvet, alkalied, had gone dry and there was no milk for Tam. "She'll get on without milk," Jared assured her, making light of it. "She's a great big girl now. She can eat and drink as the rest of us eat and drink."

It's for you I want milk, Tamsen thought. Milk and eggs and greens. You need them more than Tam does. But she gave no utterance to her anguished thoughts.

They were encamped for the night by the Green River, so pleasant and cool. For days they had looked forward to the Green River as travelers in the desert long for the oasis. In their fevered imagination it had become a mirage, green against the horizon, always just beyond their reach. Yet here they were at the Green River. They had reached it at five in the afternoon at the end of a fifteen-mile drive ankle-deep in dust, and against a wind that had whipped the dust in their faces until they looked as if they wore masks of gray clay. Tamsen had made Jared tie a handkerchief across his mouth and nose because the fine dust made him cough so. Wonderful Green River! The hundreds who had gone before them had devoured all the grass along its banks, but the water itself was there, cool, refreshing, truly green as it ran its emerald course to California.

Tonight it would be cold. Last night there had been half an inch of ice on the water buckets. Now the Wyoming sunset suddenly became night. Tamsen, clearing the tin dishes and basins and iron spoons from their supper table, looked over her shoulder for the children playing by the campfire. Jarry, with little Abner Haskins, was deep in some boys' game. "Jarry, where's Tam? Go get her. It's bedtime."

The small Jared, busy with his own devices, did not look up. "She's here." But she wasn't. Tamsen looked into the group at the next campfire, at the next; she stood up as though jerked by a cord, she stared this way and that into the dusk. Tam! Tam!

"Round by the wagons, likely," Jared said. He walked swiftly over and peered into them; called. Quickly, then, he went from group to group. "Tam here with you folks? My little girl here? Tam?" Like a crazed thing Tamsen began to run from spot to spot, her hands open and reaching ahead of her. Tam! Tam! in a voice that was high and cracked like a crone's.

They all recalled the story of the child who suddenly was missing in the McAlastair wagon train, California bound. It was as well known as the story of the Donner party. Three, the child had been, like Tam. They remembered now how that other party had called, searched; how the men had mounted and ridden in all directions; how the whole wagon train had waited a day—two days—three—four—and then had had to move on, sternly, or perish all. The mother, with another small child and a third on the way, had sat stony-faced on the wagon seat, searching the terrible horizon with dry staring eyes as the wagon rolled on toward California.

They were all on their feet now, running this way and that. Leather creaked as the men saddled their weary horses. It was the child Jarry who found her curled up asleep under a pile of buffalo robes that Eli Wheeler had left out to dry on the bank of a little knoll a hundred feet from camp.

As she held the sleepy bewildered child in her arms Tamsen began to cry hysterically. Her usually serene face worked with her agony and relief. She gripped her husband's arm with frantic fingers. "I want to go home! Let's go back, Jared. Let's go back home!"

He tried to calm her with soothing words, his arm about her and the child. But Abiah Pinney, the practical, brought her to her senses.

"You can't go back, ma'am. Why, you're in Wyoming. You're facing towards home this minute—your future home. And that's Californy."

Jacob Cobbins, the hired hand, grinned with relief and laid his great sunburned paw on the shoulder of little Jarry, the hero of the moment. "Betcher life! Ain't nobody going to turn back now, is there, Jarry! Californy or bust! Like the feller says, there's gold in them there hills."

SECOND NIGHT

JAY DISCOVERED he'd have to have his suit pressed. The porter said the valet was piled up with work and wouldn't be able to press it for a couple of hours, anyway. "God, what kind of a train is this!" Jay shouted. Everything had gone wrong. It had been discovered that Tam's sniffle was worse and she had a little temperature. The New York market reports had come in over the radio late that afternoon. Jay and his two business friends had listened with narrowed eyes and lips pursed over cigars. It had been most depressing. He had come back to Frances for comfort at six and found her still not up.

"For God's sake, France, you're not going to be carried off this train on a stretcher tomorrow morning, are you! What's the matter with you, anyway? Turned into an invalid or something?"

"Nothing's the matter with me, thank you. But there will be if you don't take that filthy thing out of this room. What's that you're smoking?"

Jay removed it from his mouth and looked at it as though seeing it for the first time. He looked at its lighted end, with the fine collar of thick gray ash. Then he put it back in his mouth, rolling it a little with his tongue and lips as he spoke.

"This, dear lady, is what's known as a cigar. Product of Cuba. Made of the tobacco plant, first brought to England, they say, by Sir Walter Ral——"

"Well, it's a nasty stinking thing, you never smoke cigars, I suppose it's those big business boys have made you go so male and Western all of a sudden." She began to sprinkle the woodsy toilet water all about the little room. "After all, I'm resting so as to have the strength to go through this wretched week we're facing. I should think you'd be delighted to have me take it this way. Perhaps you'd rather have me running up and down this miserable train swapping cooking recipes with your Mrs. Murchison while she breathes germs all over me."

He strode into his own room and slammed the door. Jerry was sitting there curled up by the window reading in the fading light. "Hello, son, what's the matter with your own room?"

"Tam's got a worse cold, I'm not allowed near her, Turkey says maybe I'd better even sleep here with you tonight. It's—uh—very con-ta-jus, colds are."

Jay threw his cigar into the cuspidor. He didn't like them, really. Jerry was deep in his book. Jay sat staring out of the window. What was the matter with everything? Fran was pretty and smart. Two swell kids. Not always enough money, but that was going to be all right now. Yet something was wrong. They all took everything for granted. He, too. Too easy, or something. Soft. He ought to be happy as hell, and he wasn't.

Jerry closed his book. The eerie whistle of the train came back to them as they hurtled across the continent. "This is a poky old train. I'd rather go in an airplane."

Jay Content was still staring out of the car window. Desert, sagebrush, mountains, the blue-gray dome of a pitiless sky. Something clicked in his memory and he saw a little wagon train plodding against the far horizon. The white-topped wagons, gray now with dust, the slow wearied pace of oxen and mules, the dwindling string of horses, the lean dogs, the underfed men and women and children, the wooden wheels grinding the sand and sinking into it, the animals' flanks dark with sweat.

"Look, Dad, tell me a story about how Great-great-great Grandfather Jared Content when he was a little boy no older than me had to drive a whole lot of oxen and mules. Gee! I'd like to do that, cracking the ol' whip, whoa there! Giddap! You won't even let me drive the pony cart alone. Go on, tell me about it. It isn't true though, is it? You just make it up."

"Of course it's true. Don't be silly. It's history. American history. No use starting a story now, though, because the train stenographer's coming in any minute. He's due now to take a lot of letters and telegrams. By the time I've finished dictating to him it'll be your suppertime, son."

"Can't you do your letters and things afterwards?"

"No. They'll have to be ready to send by air mail when we stop at Reno tonight."

"Can I see it? Reno?"

"You'll be tight asleep. One o'clock in the morning. Besides, we only stop a few minutes. Everybody 'll be asleep. There's nothing to see."

The boy wriggled impatiently. "Everybody's always busy. Just till he comes—the man who is going to fix your letters—won't you tell about it? You know—about the wagons and the Indians and the oxen, the way your father told it to you when you were a little boy, and his father told it to him."

"Well—but he'll be here any minute and I'll have to stop in the middle, and then it will be your supper-time. Let's see—uh—well, your Great-great-great Grandmother Tamsen Content, she was quite a girl. Once when they were near a place called Soda Springs—that's not far from where we are this minute on the train—an old one-eyed mean-looking cuss of an Indian with two or three other Indians behind him bounced out of the brush when the party was camped. Most of the men were off looking for game and getting water and so on. There were only a couple of teamsters left. The Indians began to pillage the wagons——"

"What's pillage?"

"Steal. They began to steal things, and the teamsters were scared out of their wits and didn't even try to fight, but Tamsen Content was in the back of her wagon and she just leaned over and went after their hands with a hatchet. They began to howl, and then the teamsters pulled themselves together and got their guns and began to shoot——"

The door buzzer sounded. "Good evening, Mr. Content. Stenographer."

THIRD MONTH

DESERT, SAGEBRUSH, mountains, the great blue-gray dome of a pitiless sky. That May day seemed so long ago, so terribly long ago, when Ambrose Haskins, newly elected captain of the wagon train, had said grimly, "High mountains, broad deserts, great rivers, and hostile Indians. It ain't those that 'll give us most grief. . . . Eighteen miles a day, rain or shine, eighteen miles a day, no matter what."

Tamsen was up in the wagon seat most of the day, now. She looked ahead toward California but her eyes no longer really saw the train of wagons, their canvas tops bleached dead white with the sun like the drying bones along the trail; the slow-pacing oxen, the dwindling string of horses, the great wheels grinding the sand and sinking into it, the animals' flanks dark with sweat.

"You all right, Jared?" she would call over her shoulder.

"I'm fine. I'm getting up in a minute now," Jared's queer thin voice from the wagon bed. Little Jarry sat beside her on the wagon seat now, and often he actually drove, though there was little enough to driving really, with these weary animals plodding ahead through the sand. Whoa! shouted little Jarry, enjoying it enormously. Whoa! Gee! Haw! Little Tam sat up there, too, or with Jacob and Lavina in the second wagon. Tam's hair was bleached almost white from the sun and wind, she was tall and thin. Too thin. All except Lavina. Lavina had grown plump, and she was ill, mornings. The wives nodded their heads and told her to eat bits of dry pilot bread to stop the morning sickness. Everyone else was thin and irritable and over-silent. There was a sort of poisonous unseen thing running through the whole wagon train. Frayed nerves, blistered feet, sunburned eyes, lips swollen and blotched with the dust as though they had tasted poison ivy; filthy alkaline water, no proper food for the animals. These and a thousand other things combined to lower the morale of the party. The Valley of the Humboldt, it was called, this long brutal killing stretch. The final heartbreaking pull before you reached California. The Valley of the Shadow, Tamsen thought, bitterly, listening to Jared's breathing, seeing how the ribs of the oxen and mules stuck out almost comically under the dust-covered hides.

How old she felt! She was fifty years older than she had been that May morning when they had pulled out of Independence, Missouri. Her fine walnut bed was gone, her precious walnut table, her iron stove—all left to rot by the roadside. Velvet was gone, killed one night by the thieving Indians. They had let her out to graze on a bit of rare green growing in the midst of an alkali stream, and an Indian arrow had got her.

Well, she had learned a lot of queer things. How smart Jared had been—was, she said, quickly, fear clutching her. Was? *Is.* That cream of tartar made this horrible alkali water drinkable. He had known that. That vinegar and tartaric acid had kept them from having the scurvy. Mule steaks were not so bad. And if you were out of salt and pepper a little gunpowder made them palatable. Jacob's accordion! In her rage and grief she had said, "Make him throw that away if I have to throw away my bed and my table and stove and iron pots and dishes and everything I love."

"We need that accordion," Jared had said. "A wagon train can do well without a bedstead and a table and even an iron stove. But the music of an accordion, evenings, can make you feel you can push on next day."

Jared knew everything. Little Jarry was like him. Smart and quiet and long-headed. Oh, God, let us get to where there's milk and eggs. Let him not die, dear God. Just milk and eggs and my good cooking and he'll be all right, and the children, too.

Dust. Sun. Jolting, racking, over the mountain roads. Eighteen miles a day, rain or shine, or you land in the snow in the High Sierras——

They should tell people how awful it was, before they ever got started. But they didn't come back to tell. They either stayed or they fell by the way. She had seen them. Crazy men and women trudging back by foot, or trying to, and dying by the way. Animals crazed with heat and drought, or dropping suddenly in their tracks without warning. She had seen them, often, in the past month, going along slowly, patiently, in this desert, and then, as if shot, they would fall and die instantly. As you passed them on the trail the desert sand in the dead animals' eyes gave them an unearthly glitter.

What had she not seen! Soda Springs; ice ponds in July; skulking Indians with poison-tipped arrows; books thrown away with other litter by the side of the trail; dust that made it impossible to see the wagon ten feet ahead of you; oxen dying in heaps; men dying of cholera; children being born on the trail; a wedding in an ox cart.

In desperation she resolved to go to Ambrose Haskins, leader and captain of the wagon train.

"Mr. Haskins—it's about Jared. He isn't sick—not really, I mean. Only tired. If we could only stop for one whole day, and rest. It's the going on, day after day, all these weeks and months without stopping. It's wearing him out. It's killing——"

"We're all of us worn out, Mrs. Content, and that's a fact. But Jared's going to pull through fine with the rest of us. Less than a month more of it, and you'll be wearing gold nuggets for a necklace."

"I want no necklace." She felt hysteria coming into her voice and was powerless to check it. "He'll die, I tell you! He'll die if he doesn't get a little rest. That terrible jolting in the wagon, or else the sun beating down on his head, walking; and the dust and alkali. It would be like heaven not to feel your bones being racked. Oh, Mr. Haskins, please, for God's sake, let him rest a day. When we make camp today or maybe tomorrow, if it's a spot where there's some water and maybe even a tree, let's stay there a day. Just a day, quiet. Please, Ambrose. Just a day, for Jared."

His voice, his face were compassionate but stern. "We can't, ma'am. You well know why." He pointed across the burning desert toward the direction of the mountains, the last barrier between them and their goal. "There's the mountains ahead of us. We've got to get over them before snowfall or we'll perish, all of us. Dust or storm, sickness or death, we must go on, eighteen miles a day. One day lost may mean a day too late. A blizzard in the mountains, and we're done for. Remember Hagar in the wilderness, ma'am. Remember Sarah, mother of nations. So will you be, mother of a nation. Strength for two, Mrs. Content, that's what you'll have to have. And let's hear no more about stopping."

She went back to the wagon. As she climbed up over the wheel she heard someone in the next cart singing a bitter parody of her favorite song:

"Oh! Susanna,
Go to hell for all of me;
We're all of us the livin' dead
Bound for Californ-i-ee."

"You all right, Jared?"

"I'm fine. I'm getting up now. I was just thinking, Tamsen. Those of us that get to Californy and settle there, we'll be fit to face anything after this. We'll be the iron it takes to dig gold. We'll be a race of giants in Californy."

"Yes, Jared."

ARRIVAL

IT HAD BEEN a ghastly scramble to be up and dressed by the time they were due in San Francisco. Seven fifty-two in the morning.

"If they dawdle around at Omaha and Reno and heaven knows where—as they did—why don't they dawdle a little longer!" Frances Content suggested, "Then we might get in at a fairly decent hour; nine o'clock, at least.

"I'll have to have a cup of coffee. Katharine, ring and tell him a cup of coffee, here. I'll die if I don't have it right away."

"They'll have breakfast waiting as soon as we get to the house," Jay called from his room.

"I know. But if I don't have coffee as soon as I'm up I get one of my headaches. You know that."

"Do I know it! Listen, tell him coffee for two, will you? I feel rotten. Maybe a cup of coffee will buck me up. I'll bet I didn't sleep two hours."

"Funny they didn't answer your last telegram."

"Maybe nothing to say. The wire at Reno said he was holding his own—whatever that means—and conscious. No change, I guess."

Frances passed through his room to the children's. She looked very smart and fresh in a dark print and a tiny turban. "Don't put their coats on yet, Miss Turck. It'll be hours. Well, half an hour, at least. . . . No,

Tam, no faces, darling. You're not sick any more. Turkey took your temperature and you haven't a speck. . . . Did they drink all their milk? They can have a good breakfast at Grandpa's. Much better than this stale train food—I hope. I had a lamb chop last night that was simply rubber. And asparagus the size of my little finger. Heaven knows I eat little enough on a train, but I do want that little decently—Jerry, what *are* you doing, shouting so, you'll be worn out before we get there."

"He's driving oxen, he says, he's been at it ever since he got up, I couldn't get him dressed he wriggled so," Turkey explained, good-humoredly enough.

Jerry's face grew red. "I'm not. Ol' fool! And you didn't! I dress myself. I aren't a baby, like Tam."

"Jared Content, don't you let me hear you talk——"

Jay stuck his head in at the door. "Coffee, France. Better swallow it. We'll be there in less than fifteen minutes."

He was feeling better this morning. Must have been a touch of indigestion made him feel so low yesterday. Too much food without exercise, and those cigars. Frances, too, was her gay vital self, bright-eyed, capable, chic.

"I've had a lovely rest. Did you see the mountains early? Divine! Jay, some time if we're—when we have—well, with the money—you know—anyway, let's go to one of those Western mountain snow resorts for the skiing, shall we? It would be fun."

"Winter, you mean?"

"Yes, way up high, where the snow's very deep and the sun hot. Mimi Bayliss went last winter. She said she never saw such luxury. Imagine! Even Mimi! Something-or-other-Lodge, it's called. Sun traps, and priceless skiing and skating and such food! The mountains in winter! Exciting!"

Jay's brother, Jacob Content, was there to meet them as they stepped off the train. Frances took one look at him and whispered a quick aside to Jay. "He's trying to look mournful, but he's really pleased about something. Grandpa Content is dead—that's it. I feel it."

He and Frances had never got on. Jacob Content did not look a Content. He favored the other side of the family; the Cobbinses, offspring of Jacob Cobbins and Lavina, the hired man and servant girl of the old '49er days. Among the first of that wagon train to strike it rich in California, it was their daughter that Jared Content had married in 1862. He's common looking, Frances thought now, as he came toward them, and slick. Jacob Content and his wife and children lived in New York. Frances resented that, too, with a fierce Chicago resentment.

"Hello, Jay," he now said somberly. "How are you, Frances. Hello, kiddies."

"It's nice of you to meet us," Frances said quickly. "How is he?"

Jacob wore the unctuous look of one who bears tidings. "I've got sad news for you. He—went—at six this morning. Adele and I were with him at the end. And the children—in the next room of course—the children."

"I'm sorry," Jay said.

Frances echoed it, hollowly. "Sorry." Then her resentment of him flared into anger. "We got here as soon as we could. We took the very first train."

Jacob Content flicked an eye at the great transcontinental monster that had hurled them across thousands of miles. "We flew."

The little procession moved toward the waiting car.

Jay Content looked a trifle dashed. "But we came." As though continuing an unspoken train of thought.

Frances was not one to beat about the bush, especially with so thick-skinned an antagonist as her brother-in-law. "The telegram said that we were to come, all of us, and that it was imperative. And we came. So they can't say—uh——"

"Oh, you're all right," Jacob assured her jocularly. "You finished at the post, and you qualify."

"Oh, say, look here!" Jay's tone was protesting.

"But now the wretched boring trip was for nothing," Frances concluded. "That is, in a way. We thought he wanted to see us all and that he'd probably live for weeks and weeks. The way he did the last time."

Jacob Content had a San Francisco morning paper in his hand. He unfolded it now. There was a three-column photograph of old Jared Content, a magnificent towering figure, rugged, keen-eyed, looking out at them with the quizzical gaze of the undeceived. But it was not to the picture that Jacob Content pointed. He indicated the headline:

CENTENARIAN '49ER
LEAVES FIFTY MILLION

Jacob Content almost smiled before he remembered he mustn't. "Oh, I wouldn't say the trip was exactly for nothing, Frances. There's gold in them thar hills."

ARRIVAL

THAT FIRST GLIMPSE of the Promised Land had come on August 15th. Somehow they could not realize it. The weeks, the months, had been too long. Through those last days the journey had had a dreamlike quality of unreality. The weary jaded wagon train had ascended painfully through forests of evergreen timber, up and up on the last stretch of the fantastic climb until they reached timber line. The trees were only stunted twisted things. The snow was old and hard as ice. They were more than nine thousand feet above sea level. The thin air seemed to agree miraculously with Jared. Sallow and peaked though he was there came a freshness into his face and movements, a sparkle into his eyes.

"But he won't be fit to do anything when we get

there," Tamsen had confided to Sarah Haskins. Her tone was not one of complaint. She spoke as though facing a fact squarely. "He couldn't dig and shovel, the way they'll have to in the gold-fields. Gold-fields. It's funny. I don't care a thing about whether there's gold or not. Just Jared, to be well again, and the children happy."

Sarah Haskins was quick to reassure her. "He'll pick up in no time now. They say the sun and the air are like wine and a tonic."

"He can hardly turn his pillow. Well, I can work. I can cook and wash and sew. Surely they'll need work like that to be done in Hangtown. Jared said he heard they were planning to change the name to Placerville. I wish they would, time we get there. It's so much nicer sounding."

North, south, east, and west lay the golden plains seen from the heights, threaded by a line of blue. Ambrose Haskins pointed with one dust-grimed finger. "That line there, it's the coast range of mountains near the Pacific. In between is the valley of the Sacramento and the Joaquin rivers. And that there beyond is the west slope of the Sierra Nevadas." The pointing hand came up above his head then in a fist of triumph. "Yessir, we've made it, by God!"

"By God," echoed Tamsen quietly.

Now they began the steep descent. Some of them rushed down the precipitous slopes. You found their wagons in a heap at the bottom, the precious belongings which they had carried over two thousand miles now strewn like debris in the dust. The thin clear air was deceptive. The diggings looked so near, though they still were days away. It was three days later that Tamsen, dragging a painful way through the dust and sun, suddenly raised her drooping head, as though listening. She was seated perched high on the driver's seat, early, early in the morning. Through the jangle of the trace chains, the grunts of the mules, the clop of the oxens' hooves, the grind of wagon wheels on dust, the shouts of the drivers, she heard a lovely sound and then another. Her face grew radiant, was transfigured as though celestial music filled the air.

Across the plains on the morning breeze was borne the sound of a cowbell. And then a cock crowed.

DATE DUE

Nov 23 65
Nov 23 65
Jul 31 67

GAYLORD PRINTED IN U.S.A.